DIARY OF INTERRUPTED DAYS

DIARY OF INTER

DRAGAN

RUPTED DAYS

TODOROVIC

RANDOM HOUSE CANADA

www.randomhouse.ca

Random House Canada and colophon are trademarks

This book is a work of fiction. Names, characters, places, and incidents
either are the product of the author's imagination or are used fictitiously.
Any resemblance to actual persons, living or dead, events, or locales is
entirely coincidental.

Library and Archives Canada Cataloguing in Publication

Todorovic, Dragan, 1958–
Diary of interrupted days / Dragan Todorovic.

ISBN 978-0-307-35688-8

I. Title.
PS8639.O36D52 2009   C813'.6   C2008-904341-3

Design by Terri Nimmo

Printed in the United States of America

10 9 8 7 6 5 4 3 2 1

For Si

DIARY OF INTERRUPTED DAYS

AN DER SCHÖNEN BLAUEN DONAU

RETURN. *April 22, 1999*

Note: I
*Most people believe that their endeavours define them. Their
striving becomes a symbol of who they are. But that is only half
of the picture. We search for some public grail to avoid a deeper,
unconfessed compulsion. In some secret place in our memories,
carefully covered, unlit, lies the truth about us: you are what
you run away from.*

Underneath he scratched the date and added "T.O." in his
hurried, slanted handwriting. He liked to locate his ideas
precisely, to know where he was when they first came to
him, and his notebooks read like maps that traced his every
move—a geography of ideas.

The light in the plane toilet turned his skin into parchment. The man in the narrow mirror ran his long, bony
fingers from the back of his shaved head down his forehead
and face to pull at his goatee, sharpening it, then did the
whole motion backwards, as if voiding his face, and then

reshaping it. He had a silver signet ring on the index finger of his right hand. He took a closer look at the man on this side of the mirror and said, "You look like a ghost, friend."

The captain's voice interrupted him. "Ladies and gentlemen, we are beginning our descent to Budapest Ferihegy Airport. Please return to your seats and fasten your seatbelts. The local time is 9:11. The weather in Budapest is good. The current temperature on the ground is ten degrees Celsius, and the skies are clear. Thank you for flying with Malév. We wish you a pleasant stay in Hungary."

Of course—he was not in Toronto, he was in midair. He crossed out "T.O." and wrote "Hung.", closed the notebook and put it back into the pocket of his black jacket. He washed his hands and returned to his seat.

From a plane most cities look like deserted beaches: the boulders of storage hangars and factories in the back, the tiny houses like pebbles that fell off the business monoliths, the hotels lined up near the water like sand castles. He watched out the window as the plane flew over the Danube, a spacious park, and then another stretch of pebbles towards the airport.

The passengers started buttoning up and putting their shoes back on. Some were combing their hair, or fixing their makeup, as if everyone on the plane had been engaged in an eight-hour debauchery and now needed to cover it up. Soon, they would all line up according to the money they had spent on their ticket: first class ahead, then business behind them, and the oh-shitters at the back. Then the door would open and everyone would be flushed into the city from this flying bowel. He gathered his magazines, folded them and pushed them inside the seat pocket in front of him. The same hysterical rant about the just humanitarian war was everywhere—he did not want to carry any of it with him.

He put his right hand in the pocket of his black leather vest and took out two passports. He opened the blue booklet and looked at his photo, then flipped the red passport open and put the images next to each other. Two faces. Two men. Two worlds. He put them back, then touched the envelope full of money tucked in the inside vest pocket. He'd brought almost everything he had with him. He would need it all. For the funeral, for the posthumous meal, to bribe the officials so they didn't grab him and put a uniform on him after the burial, to pay for the return tickets—or just in case, and there would always be a case.

When most of the passengers had departed, he stood up, opened the overhead compartment, and pulled out his old brown leather bag.

The customs officer was a young man with watery blue eyes. "Boris Bulic? What is the purpose of your visit to Hungary, sir?"

"I'm just passing through."

"Where to?"

"Farther south."

"Serbia? You won't be able to get across the border with your Canadian passport. And it might be dangerous—your country is bombing them, too."

"I have my Yugoslav passport with me."

"Are you going there to fight? Because you should hurry up. Your side will be defeated in no time."

3

"You don't know what my side is."

The blue eyes narrowed under the cap brim, regarding him, then flicked down and back, comparing the passport photo with the passenger. The passport picture showed softer features, framed with a dark untidy mane, eyes slightly amused.

"You don't look like your photo."

"I'm getting old."

"You know I could ban you from entering?"

"Under the circumstances, that might be a favour," Boris said.

The officer stamped the passport and handed it back to him.

The terminal was crowded. Boris noticed that the majority of passengers had children with them, which struck him as unusual. Most of the kids were well dressed but too quiet for their age, trailing behind their parents who pushed airport carts loaded with multi-storied piles of baggage. Bits of conversation wafting out of the crowd were mostly Serbian. Boris stopped to buy a coffee at one of the less busy stands before he went in search of the minibus to Belgrade. If it was still running.

At the door, he had to stand aside and let a group of hurried people enter before he could come out. A red stroller pushed over his foot. As soon as he stepped out of the building, he lit a cigarette. The sky was cloudless as promised. "Clear days are the worst," his mother had said on the phone from Belgrade. "When there is a storm, the planes don't come at all." He removed the lid from the cup and took a sip. An older woman in a green coat came up to him, confidentially asking, "Room, sir?" He ignored her.

The entrance to the departure hall was swarming with people. Cab drivers made short stops in front of the terminal, idling there as tired parents pulled out their offspring and their giant bags. All flights from Belgrade were suspended and Budapest was the closest airport for Serbs fleeing the war. Most people had someone drive them to the Hungarian border, then took a train or a bus from there.

Several big buses idled in the parking lot across the road, but no minibus that he could see. His friends in Belgrade had told him there was only one still making the trip between the Budapest airport and Belgrade, and that one was grey. It was up to Boris to find it: the driver didn't have much in the way of return fares and would not hang around for long at the airport after delivering his load of refugees. He'd simply refill the tank, take a short break, and drive back before nightfall.

As Boris turned back towards the main entrance, he noticed a person sitting on the pavement, leaning against one of the big pillars. His face was hidden by a baseball cap, and a cardboard sign was propped in his lap—"Budapest–Belgrade." Boris knelt beside the man and said, "Can you drive me?" In response he received a short snore. Boris decided to let the man sleep. He could finish his coffee in the meantime. There was an empty bench a few steps away. The seat was still warm.

The flow of people continued in one direction: into the building and towards the departure hall. Away. He was going back to Belgrade, but Belgrade, it seemed, was leaving. For a moment, he let a thought of finding that woman in the green coat and taking her up on her offer flutter in his mind—maybe a night or two here would help him get over jet lag and arrive fresh in Belgrade—but then he dismissed it. He knew what it was, and there was no time for weakness. Swimming against the tide, again. Good.

Boris finished his coffee and another cigarette. He couldn't wait any longer. He bent down and prodded the man, who raised his cap, wiped the saliva off his chin with the back of his hand, and looked around, confused. His dark eyes had violet shadows underneath them. Boris figured he was probably in his mid-thirties, but he looked so tired that it was hard to be sure.

"I need a ride to Belgrade," Boris said, slipping into Serbian.

"I need a coffee. Wait for me."

Boris stared after him as he entered the terminal. He thought he recognized the man. Another circle was closing. Boris liked that feeling. When circles close in one's life, when small parts of private history are repeated, it brings a sense of order and comfort. A moment when one could almost believe that there is some harmony in this cacophonic, screaming world.

The driver remained silent while manoeuvring through the busy streets of the capital, and Boris did not feel like talking, either. Sitting up front in the passenger seat, he watched the street names through the windshield, trying to remember them. He had been to Budapest several times in the old days, mostly to attend rock concerts. He and his friends would drive to the centre of town, spend some time on Váci Street, eat quickly, get high, and go to the stadium. He had once known the promenade by the Danube well, but it too had faded. Everything had faded. He wasn't even sure how Belgrade would look to him after five and a half years in Canada. Not because of the bombing. Bombs explode, but they are too big to comprehend. Devastation on a large scale never affects you in real time, even when you watch it live. Your brain refuses to take it in. You do know that something horrible is happening, something that will change you forever, but you shut down in the face of it, and just watch it, and eat, drink, sleep, fuck. Later, when your brain realizes that you are still alive, your emotional space opens and the pain comes.

He wasn't thinking of the bombs dropping on Serbia now, blowing holes in the fabric of his past, but of how different home was bound to be. That is the trouble with home—step out of it for even a second, and it will hurl itself towards other people.

He looked over at the driver, who finally seemed to be waking up and was scratching some spot between his shoulder blades with the tip of a long screwdriver. He had removed his cap in the meantime and Boris noticed a scar high on his forehead. Yes, it was him. The stubble on his cheeks was on the edge of becoming a beard. He was dressed in jeans and a corduroy jacket that used to be brown but now was the colour of wheat. Boris felt a surge of gratitude to the man for bringing him home.

"I remember you," Boris finally said. "You drove us out of the country in October 1993. But it was a different bus."

"No, it's the same one. It was red then, which was good for business. Now it's better if it's grey. To melt with the road. Us?" He glanced Boris's way, checking out the silver earring that gave Boris's shaved head the look of either artist or thug.

"My wife and me."

"She's not coming back with you? Too dangerous?"

"No, she's not afraid. Sara's . . ." Boris searched for the right words. "She's dealing with some inheritance business."

"Inheritance? That can't hurt."

"This one's messy."

They both fell silent for a while, watching the road. The last houses on the outskirts of Budapest were already behind them, and the factories, and they were driving by some small village. There were no hills in sight, and the highway appeared to curve just because it was a proper thing to do.

"My pickup point was on Slavija then, right?" the driver said.

Boris nodded.

"People loved it when I drove that one last circle around the square. I guess it felt good to leave home from the heart of the city. Now I park in front of Saint Marcus's Church— any help I can get." He laughed.

"How often do you make the trip?"

"Every day, rain or shine. Rain or bombs, rather. You've probably heard—they don't bomb on rainy days. Some say it has something to do with the electricity in the clouds. Screws up their instruments. I think it has more to do with the locators."

"Locators?"

"Their spies have placed small boxes close to the targets that send signals to the satellites. I think they're trying to avoid hitting civilians. So when it's cloudy, and they can't receive the signal from the ground, they don't fly."

"Have you seen any of these . . . locators?"

"They've shown a few on television. Small black things, hard to find. The heart of darkness."

A bus driver quoting Conrad? "What did you do before this?"

"I studied journalism at the Faculty of Political Sciences. Did some writing, too, before the war, mostly for some student magazines. Then it all went to hell. You left in 1993? Then you remember how it was: what Milosevic didn't want, he destroyed. The whole profession started sucking, if you ask me. They dug trenches and disappeared into them. From time to time someone would run from one hole into another, and that was all."

" 'Your hole is our target,' " Boris said.

"What?"

"I saw a truck in England once—it belonged to some company that specialized in drilling holes through walls. That was their motto."

"Rats. It was the time of rats, when Milosevic came to power. Underground, negative selection, running in packs, bathing in shit. When the West imposed sanctions against Serbia in 1992, all flights from Belgrade stopped, as you know. Still, people were leaving this dump in hordes. That's when I decided to do this for living. I thought what the hell, I'll borrow some money, get a minibus, drive people to and from Hungary. I figured I'd make some money in the short term, because it can't last forever. Here I am, still driving. Mostly *to* Hungary."

He scratched his scar, then continued:

"Maybe this bombing will change something. The noise, if nothing else. They are dropping some large ones, you know. Every time a bomb explodes, I think, 'There's another wake-up call.' Maybe after this I'll go back to journalism— if people wake up and change something. What do you do?"

"In Canada?"

"Is that where you live?"

"Yes."

"Doing what?"

"I'm an art director for an ad agency."

"Nice."

"Not bad."

"And before you left?"

"I was a conceptual artist."

"Really? Tell me something you did, maybe I'll remember."

"You won't."

"Try me."

"Okay. The Ice Cream Idol."

The driver pursed his lips. "Nope."

"I made a statue of Milosevic out of ice cream. It was in a big cooler truck in the Square of the Republic in Belgrade for one day only. You could destroy the idol by licking him, but then you'd have to taste him."

"Did you put a stick up his ass?"

"I felt something was missing."

They laughed.

"What else?"

"Musical Gallows. I built twelve gallows and hung dummies on them, and the ropes were harp wires, all different lengths. They each played a different tone when plucked."

"It was in the Student Cultural Centre, right? There was a fuss about it."

"It was banned. The gallows played the national anthem."

"That's why I remember it."

As far ahead as Boris could see the road going their way was empty. All the traffic except their minibus was headed towards Budapest and away from Belgrade.

"Are these cars—?"

"Yes—all escaping to the north. Some Hungarians who live on the border are moving, too. The other day a stray bomb fell on some house in Bulgaria. It's crazy back home, you'll see."

The cigarettes and coffee hadn't removed that plastic aftertaste from the plane food in Boris's mouth, and he reached for a piece of gum in his pocket. There wasn't any. "Have you had any breakfast?" he asked. "If you want, we can stop somewhere and I'll buy for both of us."

"Then we'd better do it now. The closer you get to the border, the uglier the people you meet. Some Hungarians see our misery as their chance to get rich. Farmers have converted their stables into bed and breakfasts, and they charge an arm and a leg. You go to a gas station anywhere on this road, and you pay ridiculous sums for gasoline if your vehicle has Serbian plates. By the way, I'm Miša."

Ten minutes later, Miša slowed to turn right onto a side road. They entered a village, and after taking the first left, they pulled into a parking lot in front of a small café. It was in a picture-perfect house, with white walls, green shutters, and flowers in window boxes. Miša switched off the engine and they went inside together, and took a table by the window. A petite brunette with large green eyes took their order.

"How did you find this place?" Boris asked.

"I had a flat tire once and limped in looking for a garage. The owner borrowed a spare for me, and didn't even charge. The waitress—she's the owner's daughter."

"She's sweet," Boris said.

"She is. But I come for the food. My wife hugs me each night when I get home safe, but I know that it's also so she can sniff me. And she checks my clothes for hair. It's just too complicated to stray and I can't be bothered."

Sunlight reflected on the white facades of the houses opposite the café, red and blue flowers on their windowsills. The food arrived and they ate in silence. When they were done, Boris offered Miša a cigarette.

"Which route do we take from here?" he asked as he extended his lighter.

"The usual: Szeged, Horgoš, Subotica, Novi Sad, Belgrade. It's about two hundred miles, give or take, and a little over fifty from here to the border. I always aim to get to Belgrade before five. They attack after sunset mostly, but sometimes they come sooner. In Hungary, I take it slow and steady—if the cops catch me speeding, I'm in for some serious money. After we cross the border, we'll go as fast as my bus can stand."

"Is that what you do if the planes come?"

"That's what I do. Amateurs park on the side and hide under the trees. But mice don't lie down hoping the cat won't see them." He suddenly remembered to ask: "Did your plane arrive on time?"

"No. We were an hour late. Why?"

"Fuck. Let's go."

Boris paid the girl and ran after Miša, who was already turning the vehicle around. "What?" Boris said as he closed the door and the bus veered onto the main street.

"You know how planes have to fly through certain corridors? There are roads up in the sky, just like down here. Some of those roads are in the way of the bombers. When a plane is late, it usually means that its normal corridor is closed and the bombers are coming sooner. We have to hurry."

Sara had already been gone when the bombing of Serbia started, and Boris's world had turned surreal. As an artist, he deconstructed reality and reinserted pieces intended to create a shift in perception in those who saw his art. But now nothing seemed real enough to deconstruct. He would turn up every morning at his job on the twenty-ninth floor of a building at the intersection of Yonge and Bloor, and he would try to work, concentrating on shapes and colours, lines and shades, and then find that hours had passed as he stared out the window at the CN Tower. A similar tower had already been destroyed in Belgrade. Sometimes he envisioned a giant condom covering the whole edifice, turning it into a colossal penis aimed at any deity allowing this nightmare to happen. Whenever he put his headphones on and inserted a music CD into his

Mac, he ended up searching instead for radio news on the Internet.

When he pulled into the big underground garage in his apartment building at night, he judged its merits as a shelter from air raids. On the supermarket shelves, he only had eyes for canned foods. He returned from a trip to the drugstore to buy shaving oil with band-aids and antiseptic cream. He melted sedatives under his tongue several times a day, and took Saint John's wort before he climbed into bed, but slept only a few hours each night.

He was safe in Toronto, far from the fury of metal that was happening in the Balkans. He also knew that his parents would be fine. His father was a retired general, after all, with access to the best shelters. Still, he felt that everything was being destroyed. He had been abroad long enough to start perceiving his homeland as an idea, not a set of particular people and buildings—still it was an idea buried in the foundation of his being. Each building the NATO bombers hit was part of the idea. Every time he heard of another bombing, he felt physically ill. His neck and shoulders turned to stone.

Boris thought of going back to Belgrade, but he knew he would be drafted immediately. He talked with his mother almost every day on the phone—he always expected to hear bombs exploding in the background, but never did. They had moved to their cottage an hour south of Belgrade for the duration. They had enough food and his father had brought his whole collection of weapons and ammunition with him, even a sniper rifle he obtained through channels. His mother sounded upbeat and he had no doubts about his father's mood, although, of course, they never spoke.

For the first time in years he made a steady stream of phone calls to his old friends in Belgrade, who all talked fast, describing crazy things—how terrific all-night parties were taking place in several of the larger shelters, how people brought drugs with them, and booze, how people had sex and made jokes about the bombing, how everyone had a badge with a target drawn on it. How everyone prayed for their enemies to come on foot, so they could give vent to their frustration.

In the beginning, the bombing victims were just people, somewhere, just numbers. Then, during the second week, they were people with names, people friends of his friends knew. By the third week, they were colleagues.

Boris's mentor died. The old artist was staying with his family in a city that had not been bombed at all. One night, the raptors finally came to destroy a factory on the edge of the town. The artist was three days short of his ninetieth birthday, and during his lifetime had seen both world wars and the Balkan wars. He was almost completely deaf and mostly blind and did not hear the first few explosions. But then they dropped a large one, and a trace of that horrific sound reached what remained of his hearing. Jolted out of his silence, he asked what the noise was. "It's a bomb, Grandpa!" his granddaughter replied.

"Not another war," he said, and died.

At his funeral the air-raid sirens sounded, and everyone abandoned the coffin except one man, himself old enough not to be afraid of dying.

Boris knew that his mentor's name would not be added to the list of victims, he knew that the cynical NATO spokesman would not be apologizing for this death, the way he ironically apologized for other blunders.

Then came the fourth week, and in the chess of death a move that found Boris on a bad square.

The border was close now. Miša switched the radio on and fumbled with the dial, checking for news bulletins. When all he could find was music, he relaxed a little bit.

"I've been meaning to ask you," he said, "why are you all in black?"

"I'm going to a funeral. My father died."

"From the bombing?"

"Not directly, no."

His father, ever vigilant, had got into the habit of borrowing a horse from a neighbourhood farmer. It was a workhorse, rarely used for riding, and the animal hated having someone on its back—but that's precisely what had attracted the General to it, his mother said. The owner did not mind lending the mare: he thought that it was the rider who was in danger, not the horse. The General would mount the horse, avoiding its teeth as it tried to bite his leg, and take it for a slow ride among the vineyards on the hill above the village. He would carry his binoculars and his old shotgun, and put on the jacket of his old uniform, claiming that it was the only thing that could protect him from the wind up there, on the hill. The villagers started addressing him as Marshall.

On a sunny afternoon, the General rode uphill some

time after five. The horse returned home alone just before six. While they were gone, a huge formation of bombers from Italy had flown over, going south towards Kosovo. The planes may have scared the horse or some animal had run out of the bushes to startle it. The villagers found the General lying under a pear tree. He was alive, but semi-conscious and breathing with difficulty. It took the ambulance an hour and a half to get to him, and almost three hours to drive him to the military hospital in Belgrade—another group of bombers had started attacking the capital in the meantime and the roads had been closed. The General was pronounced dead on arrival. The autopsy showed that a broken rib had punctured his lung and caused internal bleeding.

Like every other bit of news about the General from the past ten years, Boris had heard this from his mother. Boris and his father had stopped talking to each other in 1989, and there were a few years before that when they hardly talked at all. After Boris had moved to Toronto he'd rarely even thought of his dad, and when he did, it was always as the General. The General who went into politics after retiring. The General whose party was directly responsible for his son's leaving the country, like tens of thousands of others, all young, educated people, artists, doctors, engineers. The General whose political convictions were more important to him than his only son.

"This grandpa from my building, he's been through the big war," Miša said. "He told me he'd prefer to die than see enemy soldiers on our streets again."

"They will never come down from the skies."

"I don't think so, either." Miša sighed. "That's frustrating. Or maybe that's good. Perhaps our dicks are not as long as we think they are."

The music on the radio was some Croatian song, recorded before the war.

"They're playing that now?" Boris asked.

"It's as if nothing ever happened." Miša paused. "People are trying hard to forget that there was a war at all. As if all of it was just an incident caused by the drunken guests in a Balkan bar. I know some people who were in Bosnia and Croatia—they all claim they shot in the air or they didn't aim. Who did the killings, then? Maybe they're not lying, maybe mujahideen came, and mercenaries, such scum."

"We wish," Boris said. "My best friend was in Croatia for just a few weeks. He saw some ugly stuff that our boys did."

"What happened to him?"

"Deserted one night. Then left the country."

"He must have seen something he shouldn't have."

Boris didn't answer. *My best friend. Johnny.* It came so naturally.

They rode in silence. Half an hour later, they saw the customs sign on the side of the road. There was only one car ahead of them, and they were soon at the booth. The single duty officer nodded at Miša, looked curiously at Boris, and stamped their passports. The same procedure was repeated on the Serbian side, and they were through.

The General had retired in 1986 in a regular renewal of the commanding cadre. He went gracefully—got his gold watch, his decorations, and his farewell party. Still, it hit him hard. He used to say how he could hardly wait to leave the army so he could go hunting, play chess, read all the history books he had piled in his study over the years that he never had the time for. Boris remembered the large old bookcase full of red tomes behind the pompous writing desk in his father's study, a place he rarely entered. The classics of Marxism, Tito's collected works and some leather-bound volumes of the regime's favourite authors. One whole row was full of books in Russian—the lowest shelf behind locked doors. Those who had showed their support for Stalin went to jail after the country refused to enter the Eastern bloc, so the General was discreet about his love for Russian literature. Even when Boris advanced to the grade level in which Tolstoy, Yesenin, Sholokhov, and Gorky were on his reading list, his father refused to lend him his copies—he had translations as well as the originals—giving him money to buy his own.

During the first few months after he retired, the General indeed took to reading, approaching it as if it were his new job. He got up at five in the morning, had a shower, shaved, and made his first coffee. Then he read the newspapers in the living room for an hour. After a breakfast and his second coffee, he went into his study, where he would sit at his desk with a book opened flat in front of him, his notebook positioned a little to the right, his golden fountain pen next to it. He would put his glasses on, and begin to read, and wouldn't get up until one, when Boris's mother called him for lunch.

Later, in Canada, when exile edited his list of new friends without regard for his personal prejudices, Boris for the first time had the chance to spend more time with engineers of different kinds, and he saw the same need for precision in them.

It was so noticeable he wondered whether there were only two types of human brains in this world: that of an engineer (or soldier, or scientist) and that of an artist. Gender didn't seem to influence the mindset, nor class, nor colour of skin or ethnicity. Engineers wanted to measure and polish everything until it was perfect, and then they wanted to preserve it in that final state. Artists wanted to make jazz of everything. Late, disorganized, insecure, sensitive to the point that they seemed mostly incapable of communicating in any language. If you could find a brilliant engineer and a brilliant artist of exactly the same IQ, same age, and same background, put them in the same room, and put only one object in front of them, they would each describe different things. Yet both moved the world: one in seconds, degrees, radians; the other in reflections, hints, wisps.

For months, his father read—but then cracks in his concrete schedule started to appear. He would come out of his room to fill his coffee cup or to make a telephone call. Then he stopped altogether. In the late fall of 1987, he began leaving the apartment as soon as he had finished his morning newspapers, always checking his watch before he left, as if he did not want to be late. Then he started holding sessions at home with some of his old soldier friends. They went into his study and stayed there for hours, talking in subdued voices. Then new faces started appearing at those meetings.

Boris was already at the door one day when the elevator opened and a tall man stepped out. He was a legendary theatre director, also the son of a general, whom Boris had met several times during his art studies. They had even talked one time about Boris designing one of his shows, but that had never happened.

Confused, Boris extended his hand. "Hello, Maestro. Are you looking for—?"

"You? Not this time. I'm meeting with some people in 11B—" He saw the number on the open door behind Boris, and added, "Oh, I guess I'm seeing your father, then." He smiled a little awkwardly. Boris moved aside. "Have fun," he said, and headed for the elevator. He was late for his own meeting at the Student Cultural Centre.

So his father had entered politics. The director had just become a member of the United Left, a new party made up of ex-communists. Everybody in Belgrade's artistic circles talked about his betrayal: he had clashed with the communist regime all his life but now he had become one of the new apparatchiks.

An hour later, sitting at the brainstorming session for a new collective project that would ridicule both the famous director's new party and Milosevic's Socialists, Boris suddenly realized: his father and him—direct enemies now.

That project, titled "Giant Shadows of Little Men," turned out to be difficult to execute and—for one reason or another—opened in the Happy Gallery on a Sunday in February 1989, several months late. The idea was to toy with genealogy, to ridicule the nationalists who claimed that Serbs were among the oldest peoples on earth. One artist enlarged the image of a single amoeba and turned it into a passport photo. Another exhibited a broken fork— sculpted in stone—with the caption, "An early Serbian fork; 1200 BC." Boris chose to manipulate pictures from his family album: in one collage, his grandfather was a priest with a large cross on his chest and a Hitler moustache; in another his mom was addressing a Communist Party congress, her fist raised, in full red regalia. The General was there, too, a child riding a white horse through the streets of liberated Belgrade at the end of World War II, the masses ecstatic, carnations falling on his head. The nationalist media immediately and satisfyingly attacked the exhibition, calling the artists either traitors or internationalists— equally bad in a country crossbreeding xenophobia with paranoia. Only one independent magazine published an affirmative review, and the author heaped kudos on Boris's work. A couple of days later, Boris came home late to find an envelope leaning against the lamp on the desk in his room. Inside was a letter from his father:

> Boris, you have sold us, your family, your parents, for a
> little piece of dubious glory. I hope you will find
> support among your peers, because we cannot give it
> to you anymore. We have nothing to talk about.

Boris moved out that same night, a suitcase in one hand, a large black portfolio of his drawings in another. He stayed for a week with Johnny, then found a small studio, the first of several he would rent during the next few years. He was lucky that Johnny was not on tour the night he left home.

He was lucky that a few months earlier he had done a cover design for Johnny's most successful album ever, and that Johnny and he had become friends. He was lucky to meet Johnny's girlfriend, Sara, that night. Her face was familiar: she worked in the news department of Belgrade TV. She and Johnny had been together for three years already, but Boris had never met her until he turned up homeless on Johnny's doorstep. Later he wondered why it was Johnny he had turned to. Some of his colleagues had studios—he could have crashed there, and stayed longer. Was it because Johnny had meant burning, and not slow release? Or because Boris had wanted to exit his world and step into an unknown? Or because he had known, only five minutes after he had first met Johnny, that the two of them would be best friends forever?

Several miles into Serbia, Miša pulled off the road to park behind a small white car. The car's driver got out—he wore a large badge with a target on it—and opened his trunk, which was full of canisters of gasoline. He shook Miša's hand then filled the minibus tank. As Miša and Boris drove away, the man waved at them.

"You can't find gas anywhere except with guys like him," Miša said. "I used to carry my own canisters, but I don't want to ride on a bomb."

Miša was not joking when he said that once inside Serbia he would drive as fast as he could. The old engine roared as they blasted along, occasionally swerving into the on-coming lane to avoid bumps. As the day grew older, the traffic slowed. The road was empty in both directions.

Miša had to yell over the revving engine. "I saw the demonstrations in Toronto on television when the bombing started. Were you there when they set the American consulate on fire?"

"I saw the man who did it," Boris said. "He was masked, and had one of those Palestinian scarves around his head. He passed me in the crowd, holding something tight under his jacket. A minute later the fire broke out."

"So who was he then, a provocateur?"

"I don't know, but the Serb protesters never wore those headscarves."

"The Americans deserved it."

"What was the point? After that the cops put up concrete barricades and moved us to the other side of the street. And there were so many cameras on the roofs around us that I'm sure none of us will need a passport photo ever again."

"Forty minutes to Novi Sad," Miša said, pressing harder on the gas as the old minibus engine revved higher.

Like most women married to army officers, Boris's mother was a homemaker in the truest sense of the word. She was halfway through her university studies—French language and literature—when she met the General. Soldiers attack head on, full force, and they were married six months later. The first few years were hard times. His father served in remote areas and was often posted from town to town. But he moved up the ranks quickly and, finally, they were able to settle in Belgrade in a large, sunny apartment in an old building confiscated from some industrialist after World War II.

His father's friends were other officers who often visited with their wives. These women were all similar—handsome, but quiet and obedient—as if there were a prescribed type that a high-ranking officer was supposed to marry. None of them worked. Their husbands earned almost as much as the country's political leaders and their power seemed limitless. When he had achieved his rank, Boris's father had helped his relatives find jobs, get better apartments, get good loans from banks. Perhaps the only thing his father was never allowed to do was to travel abroad. Several times he went on business trips to Russia and Czechoslovakia, but the family spent their holidays on the Adriatic coast.

Boris started travelling without his parents when he was a teenager, always to the West. At first, he behaved like every other Yugoslav tourist, shopping relentlessly, returning with dozens of records, jeans, and new sneakers. Later, when he was studying fine arts, he spent most of his time in museums and galleries. His favourite one was the Alte Pinakothek in Munich. That's where he was first hit by an El Greco.

When Boris turned eighteen, his father gave him a trip to Amsterdam as a present. On the highest shelf in a dusty bookstore run by an old Russian Jew near a canal in the red-light district, he found a rare edition of Solzhenitsyn's *Gulag Archipelago* and thought that it would be a nice way of saying thank you. The book was bound in leather and it had obviously changed hands many times before ending here: the cover was creased and rough like a wise old face. He hid it in his luggage when he returned to Belgrade because he wasn't sure whether it was prohibited in Yugoslavia as it was in Russia—he believed it was.

His father took the package, unwrapped it, thanked him curtly and put the book on a shelf in the living room next to the romantic literature his mother kept on display for her friends. Compared to the books around it, which were neat and looked brand new, the Solzhenitsyn looked out of place. In poor taste.

When they sat together as a family for lunch—rarely, because Boris found myriad excuses not to take part—that book stared at him from the shelf. At first Boris thought his father put it there because the book was worn out and he loved his books untouched by anyone except himself. Once, when he was alone at home, he took it to the old bookbinder on the Boulevard of Revolution, to see if the cover could be fixed, or a new one made. The old man took the book in his hands, looked at it carefully from all sides, opened the cover, took one look from the top, and said, "This was done by a master. Keep it as it is, son." Boris carried it home and put it back on the shelf.

Several months later he finally read the book, and it became clear to him why his father had segregated the *Gulag* from the rest of his books. The General wanted his Russia to remain virginal. The book with the wise face screamed of murder and rape and pillage, and threatened to fill his utopia with cadavers. After that, Boris purposely chose a place at the table so that the book was just behind him: This is me, and this is not your Gorky.

Even in the middle of the General's reading fever, six

years later, *Gulag* remained intact on the same shelf, among the books that were never consumed.

"Look at these fields," Miša said. "Look at the cherries, the apples. Everything is blooming unbelievably this year. Some old folks say it always happens in the war years here."

The orchards on the left were covered in soft pink and white clouds. Cotton puffs full of powder from the woman in the sky.

Miša slowed down and reached for the pack of cigarettes that Boris had left on the dashboard.

"Do you mind?"

"No, go ahead," Boris said.

"Honestly, that's what keeps me here. This greenery around us. I keep staring at the trees, who tell me, 'It will be okay. All will be good again.' "

"When you make the run to Budapest, do you ever think of not coming back?"

Miša answered very quickly, and by that speed Boris knew that he was lying.

Boris looked at his watch. Two-ten.

On the May Day weekend the year Boris turned thirteen, the General took him on an outing to a military training ground outside Belgrade. The General and several of his high-ranking colleagues and their sons were gathering for a party put on by the old friend who ran the garrison.

After meeting up in the Soldiers' Club, they all climbed into a brand-new olive-green bus. A few of the older boys talked happily about the last such party, but Boris and the other younger children were mostly silent, not knowing what to expect. Twenty minutes later, the bus stopped and they got out. The weather was beautiful, Boris remembered. His mother made him wear the new brown sweater she had bought for him from a woman who had smuggledit in from Italy. It was too warm, but he didn't dare take it off, because everyone else was buttoned up. The father-officers led their sons towards a group of soldiers standing by wooden crates that held ammunition and rifles. In the field in front of them were targets, some concentric circles and others shaped like men. This was the rifle range. Boris started to perspire. That sweater.

Joking among themselves, the fathers each picked out new shiny rifles and went to the left side of the range. The soldiers, looking stern or maybe just a little nervous, distributed rifles to the boys and led them to the right, where they instructed the boys to lie down on the pieces of tarpaulin that were laid along the shallow trenches. Each boy was given instructions on how and when to shoot. The rifle was heavy, the stock was a little too big for Boris's hand, but it still felt nice to hold it. Then a corporal raised a red flag, and the firing started. On the left side, the fathers let loose long, heavy bursts of fire, like a rowdy flock of woodpeckers. The wooden silhouettes split into pieces and new ones appeared in their place. Boris held his rifle tight, aimed, held his breath—he felt cold on his stomach through the tarpaulin—and fired. Again. And again.

Their fathers eventually left off shooting to stand behind their sons as the soldier read out the results.

Boris was by far the worst shooter of them all, worse than the younger children, even the boy who was only eleven and who needed the soldier who stood next to him to step on his rifle so the stock wouldn't hit him. His father smiled and joked with the other fathers about it, but Boris knew he wasn't too happy.

Lunch was served right there on the field, beans and bread. After lunch, they walked a few hundred yards to a pockmarked area where there were deeper trenches. They were told to form a line and be very attentive: they were each about to throw a hand grenade. Not the real thing, a moustachioed sergeant explained—they contained only a fraction of the explosives—but they were still capable of blinding someone.

Boris's stomach was making odd noises. It was from that coldness in the trenches, and maybe from beans. He couldn't get diarrhea now, not here, in the world of men he had just entered for the first time.

One by one, the boys went into the trench, where the sergeant handed over a grenade. Each boy then removed the security pin, activated the grenade, and threw it towards the wooden model of a tank that stood some twenty yards away. Most of them couldn't throw it that far, but they were given points for style.

Boris was in the middle of the line. By the time it was his turn he was sweating profusely. He felt it was out of the question to refuse to do it, sighed, and stepped down into the trench. He must have been very pale because the sergeant asked him if he was all right. He nodded and took the grenade in his hand, surprisingly heavy for such a small thing. Boris still remembered the feel of his wet palm clenched around the metal pear. When he unscrewed the security cap and knocked the ignition capsule against a stone as instructed, he felt a jolt of terrible fear. He cocked his arm back behind his shoulder so forcefully the grenade flew out of his hand backwards, towards the other children in the line. The sergeant jumped on Boris, everyone hit the ground, and four seconds later, four years later, the grenade went off with a short, loud hiss. It was not only a dummy, it was defective.

The rest of the boys did not get their chance to throw. Instead they were all loaded onto the bus and driven back to the garrison. His father did not say a word to him.

Entering Novi Sad, Boris could not see any damage around them.

"I told you they are using locators," Miša said when he asked. "They are targeting bridges and selected factories. The army is down south, hidden somewhere, and in-Kosovo—that's where they don't aim much."

People on the streets seemed to be behaving as usual. He hadn't known what to expect exactly, but he thought he would see men and women dragging sacks of flour, or boxes of food, something like that. What he saw were people sitting on the patios, at the sidewalk cafés, minding their own business.

"I've seen pictures of some folks standing on bridges in Belgrade, protecting them with their lives," he said.

"That only happened once," Miša said, "and it was a bunch of retards, or maybe some prisoners, I don't know. On the first day of the bombing. Who would be crazy enough to do that?"

The oh-shitters.

Boris heard that term for the first time after the agency had won a contract worth seven million dollars. The bosses were so happy they called a meeting so that the team who made the pitch could explain how they did it.

"The target audience for this project was the oh-shitters," said Chris, the data miner on the team. "If you don't understand what I'm saying, don't worry—we coined the term especially for this pitch. Oh-shitters are people in their late forties to mid-fifties. They see an ad for savings, or that there's a new all-time high for the lottery, and they suddenly realize how old they are and that they have no money to retire on. And they say, 'Oh shit, I have to do something!' So they go for the shortcut—the lottery, or murder, or sudden marriage—it all depends. We call someone who wakes up from his stupor in a flash and tries to do something about his life—but it's already too late— an oh-shitter."

Boris immediately hated the word with such a passion that he mumbled an excuse about a headache and escaped the room. He went out for a smoke, and stayed out until the meeting was over.

Sara and he talked about it at home, later that evening. She was as bothered as he. "What is wrong with people trying to fix their lives at any time, even one day before their deaths?"

"Think of us," Boris said. "The way my colleagues reason, we came here from Belgrade too late in our lives. The best we can hope for is to have the feeling that we're secure, not any kind of actual security. We are bound to try lotteries of all sorts. Hell, our coming here was a lottery and every day on our calendar is another number in the drum. So we're oh-shitters, too. All immigrants are."

After that incident on the rifle range, something between Boris and his father permanently changed. It was like their dialogue was now edited. The General never asked again about his school sports or offered to take him to any event that was related to the army. They continued to talk about the books that Boris read, though, and he became a voracious reader. For him, books were not about the art of writing but about the talent for building: they were cathedrals of mind, tunnels of love, bridges of despair, roads of whispers. He often wanted to draw the images that the pages left in his mind, and around the time of the incident with the grenade he started doing it. In his second year of high school (he was sixteen), his art professor told him that he was good enough to study painting. But Boris did not tell his parents that he had decided to follow this advice until after his father had placed *Gulag* on the shelf. That autumn Boris enrolled at Fine Arts.

By the time he was in his early twenties, there was nothing about the son that the father approved of—not his choice of studies, or his friends, or destinations, or projections for the future. There was little help from his mother in all this. She was always on Boris's side, but secretly. She never dared oppose the General's opinions.

That was unimaginable. There was only one commander in the house.

Boris finished his studies a year before his father retired. As he started to participate in group exhibitions, the gap between his father and him became so wide that at times it seemed they spoke different languages. The General did not understand what Boris did and did not want to understand. "Is that what we fought for," he complained, "so you boys can make fun of everything?" Boris was often on the verge of reminding his father that he did not fight at all in the Second World War—being only thirteen when it ended—but he did not want to go there. Or did not dare go there—he was still living with his parents, and wasn't earning enough to go solo. Besides, he had already learned that a layer of frustration makes a good medium for art.

What surprised him, though, was that his mother only came to see his first few exhibitions. Then she started finding excuses, and finally gave up on the excuses, too. She continued to brag about him in front of her friends, but she had chosen her side.

"Someone stole my watch at the station in Belgrade. Can you imagine the dickheads—we are being bombed and they are stealing? What's the time?"

"Half an hour after the last time you asked."

"What do you say we make a break here in Novi Sad, before we cross the river, and have an espresso?"

Boris nodded, and Miša turned onto a side street, then another one, and finally parked his vehicle close to the

Danube. They found a café with a view of the river, sat on the patio and ordered their drinks. Boris stretched out his legs, lit a cigarette, and looked along the river at the remains of a bridge. Only the abutments at each end were still standing. On the hill across the river, the old Petrovaradin citadel looked as if it were made of candy: the marzipan headquarters, the marshmallow garrison, the meringue tower, the gingerbread walls.

"Miša, how long do you think you'll keep on driving this route?"

Miša stared at the demolished bridge. "As long as there are roads. I have two kids. The boy is seven, the girl three. She has asthma and takes aminophylline. I get it from abroad because our drugstores often don't have it. I need both the money from driving and the connections."

A tall young man brought their espressos.

"Here, let me get this," Miša said, then asked the waiter, "Brother, is the bridge still okay?"

"Žeželj? It's damaged, but you can still pass."

"Was it quiet this morning?"

"Yeah. Not a sign of them." The waiter took Miša's money and turned to the next table.

They drank their coffee in silence.

"Let's go, friend," Miša finally said. "Another hour and we'll be home."

Back at the minibus, Miša opened the hood to check the oil and radiator levels, closed it and got back in the cabin. He reached into the glove compartment, took out a cloth, and wiped his hands. Boris opened his bag to search for his toothbrush. He had a suspicion he had forgotten it in

Toronto, but there it was. Miša turned the key. Nothing happened. He tried again, cursing. Nothing.

"Electrical," he said, opening his door. "I must have touched the wrong wire. Stay inside, it'll be quick."

He lifted the hood again and Boris heard him banging some part of the engine. Then his head appeared from underneath the hood. "Try now."

Boris leaned to the left and turned the key. The engine started.

Miša slammed the hood, climbed back into his seat, and pumped the gas a few times. The motor roared, and he eased the pressure, shifted, and they were on the road again.

It took them five minutes to reach the bridge. It was some five hundred yards long—two elegant arches that touched in the middle of the river. Several policemen stood at an improvised checkpoint, turning all cars back. Miša slowed to a crawl, then stopped.

"Hi, guys."

"Hello, sir. Where are you going?"

"To Belgrade. I'm returning from Budapest."

Another officer who'd been standing by a police car noticed the minibus and came over to them. "Hi, Miša," he said, lightly touching the brim of his cap. "Another round, you lunatic?"

"You know how it is, brother, the smart ones are leaving and the fools are helping them."

The policeman laughed. "Okay, you can go this one time, but you have to find another route. I might not be able to let you through again. We've been ordered to let only emergency vehicles pass. I think our generals presume that if no one drives across it, the criminals won't bomb it. This being the only bridge still standing . . ."

"Thanks, man. I owe you one." Miša shifted into first gear and left it there as they crept forward. Boris soon saw why: there were cracks in the asphalt starting about a hundred yards from the bank. They were alone on the bridge. It was probably too dangerous for more than one vehicle at a time to drive over. Miša swerved left and right, trying to avoid the cracks, but it was not always possible. Then, some two hundred yards from the far riverbank, the engine coughed once, and died. Miša tried the ignition, but nothing happened.

"Can you believe this shit?"

"What do we do now?" Boris said.

"Well we can't call a tow truck. I have to fix it."

They both got out. Miša grabbed his toolbox from the back of the minibus, opened the hood, and started fiddling with a screwdriver. Boris walked a few yards to the railing, then turned to Miša. "Is it okay if I take a look at the city? I'll just be over there," he said, pointing to a spot where the arches dived towards the river, leaving a good view.

"I don't need you here," Miša said. "But don't go too far. I hope I'll be able to fix this fast."

It was strange to stand on a deserted bridge. There were no birds. The city was far enough away that the gurgle of the Danube overrode its constant hum. Small rivers are leafy-green, and bigger ones turn greyish. This river had that steely surface of power. He started whistling, quietly. *An der schönen blauen Donau*. Strauss, what else. Not *The Blue*

Danube. It was *On the Beautiful Blue Danube.* Boris smiled. Of course the river was never blue, but for court artists everything had to be *schön* and *blau.*

He looked back. Miša still had his head under the hood.

Boris leaned over the railing. The sun appeared behind one of the clouds that hung above the city as if forgotten from yesterday, and his shadow stretched out towards the Petrovaradin fortress. The shadows of the railings made his silhouette look like it was behind bars. He stared at it, thinking there was a seed of a new project right there. Perhaps something about reality not being three-dimensional but a flat projection onto the minds of others. Or something about the light. Maybe there should be bars on a wall of pure white light. Dark vertical areas that would make the wall look taller.

Behind him, in the distance, was Amsterdam. After the funeral, after he got his mother to Canada, he would leave her safe in their apartment in Toronto and travel to Amsterdam to explain everything. Or perhaps he should leave his mother in Budapest for a few days and go to Holland before going home. Right. That was better. He owed both Sara and Johnny an explanation.

He started walking away from the bus, his hands in the back pockets of his black jeans. Down there, on the surface of the river, his shadow was walking behind bars.

Strange, there were no birds at all.

He heard Miša rev the engine. He should go back. Or maybe Miša could just pick him up. The roaring went up and down, up and down—what was the man doing to his minibus? Perhaps he needed help.

Boris turned around. Miša was in front of the minibus, waving one hand towards the city behind them, beckoning with his other.

It took Boris several seconds to understand that what he had heard was not the engine of the small grey bus that melted with the road. It was the sound of a distant air-raid siren.

BLACK SNOW FALLING

DECONTAMINATION. *September 6, 1992*

"Okay, guys, can we stop the siren, please?"

The teenagers who had climbed onto the large bronze horse in the Square of the Republic, ashamed by the sudden attention of tens of thousands people upon them, turned the handle on the siren a few more times, then let go. Boris and Sara laughed at the sight of the grins on the kids' faces morphing into blank stares as they tried to become invisible.

The man behind the microphone absentmindedly picked the strings of his Stratocaster. "We don't need sirens to tell them they should run into shelters—that they should hide in the darkness, where they belong."

He was tall, his big forehead creased by a few deep lines, three-day stubble on his square chin. His long black hair curled around the shoulders of his red leather jacket.

The seed of a melody started protruding through his strumming.

"They should crawl back under a stone with their horrors."

A single female scream came from the crowd in front of the stage. Some other girl copied it way in the back, an echo of the first one. The drummer hit the bass pedal— one shot.

"They should be afraid of us."

Shot.

"Very afraid."

Shot.

"Because we have family over there. We have sisters in Zagreb, we have brothers in Sarajevo, we have our people there. And they are shooting at our people."

A salvo of shots, and a gust of wind twisted a lock of hair over the man's eyes.

"Not in our name!"

The crowd roared—"Johnny, Johnny!"—many raising their fists in the air. The drummer locked into the beat, the stormy bass followed, and Johnny flipped the middle switch on his guitar. The pickups held the last few notes he had played, distorting them. People in the first few rows, recognizing the song, started screaming and jumping. The wave lifted Sara and she began to dance beside Boris where they stood, a little to the right of the stage. Johnny grabbed the microphone stand, slid it up the strings of his guitar, and set his fury free:

Off the leash
They're coming
Ravenous and angry
To break your personality
Saltier than the sea

I am the Angel of Revenge
My destiny is my lover
As with the people, so with the priest
As with the servant, so with his master.

The blazing sound devoured the Square of the Republic, banging against the museum on the other side, shaking the framed heads inside, ricocheting and exploding onto the surrounding streets. The sea of people filling every foot of the space became turbulent. Handwritten banners saying "NO to the War" and "Not in Our Name!" were raised high, as at least half of eighty thousand people sang every verse with Johnny. At the break he tortured the solo that everyone loved into a series of spastic, frantic chords, out of tune, out of rhythm, his left hand stretching the strings to their limit, creating pain and murderous wrath. People dancing close to the stage stopped dead under the onslaught, and some started crying. The crowd wanted to tear off their skin and bite into their veins, but Johnny made them sing with him, chopping his guitar and raising his fists, his long black hair wrapped around his head like Medusa, his navel exposed to the crowd.

I am the Angel of Revenge
My destiny is my lover

The band behind him speeding towards the climax, he hit a monster chord, then slid his fingers down the neck. Multiplied by the powerful, slow echo, his guitar sounded like the night itself screaming. The crowd erupted into a sustained roar.

As Johnny and the band left the stage, a young woman stepped to the microphone, but the crowd was so loud even the large speakers behind her did not help. She tried to speak several more times but the chanting did not stop, and she glanced offstage to look for Johnny. He ran back onto the stage, took the microphone from her hand, and waved to the audience to be silent.

"This is Belgrade," he said. "This is 1992. Happy nations are preparing for the twenty-first century. Buddhists did it five hundred years ago." He rode the small wave of laughter, then hushed it. "But we live in fear and isolation. Because one man has decided that our friends of yesterday are our targets today. We want to send them a message: You are not alone. This is not happening in our name. We love you, because we understand you, and you understand us. We talk the same language, our governments do not. You stop yours, we'll stop ours, and together we shall overcome."

He panned the crowd, waiting for applause to subside.

"I won't tell you today to love one another. You know that. And I won't tell you what to do. You know that, too. But I will tell you this: We are here together now but it's only temporary. This protest will end and you will go home. You will be alone there because your fathers and your mothers are not on your side. It's not easy to fight alone.

"Do not expect glory in this. Don't fight for fame, don't fight so a street can be named after you one day—the only real heroes are the unknown heroes. Instead fight for you. Fight for us. Because if you don't, you won't be able to tell your children where you were when the war started. And if you have to lie about your past, then what kind of future do we have? We need to scream until the whole world can hear us: Not in my name!"

The crowd roared the slogan after him, raising their fists. He kissed the girl next to him on the cheek, then gave her back the microphone and left the stage.

As Sara and Boris started retreating towards the bookstore at the back of the stage, where the organizers had set up their headquarters, she whispered, "I'll just run to the washroom," and she darted ahead.

In a minute, Boris saw the crowd parting in front of Johnny, and he stepped forward. "Nice, Che, and now let's go to Fidel's for a drink." He slapped his friend's shoulder.

Johnny laughed. "Where's Sara?"

"She went to scare off your groupies."

"I have to do a short interview, then we can all go somewhere for a drink. It won't take long."

Johnny started making his way through the backstage crowd, accepting hugs and handshakes left and right and trying to move as fast as he could. Boris, following, intercepted a plastic cup with beer aimed at Johnny. "I'm his official taster," he said.

A politician was now onstage, thanking the protesters for turning out. Boris waited in front of the bookstore so he could finish off the beer. It was a good and peaceful protest; it felt for a moment as if the city had been thoroughly washed and decontaminated.

Four men in their early twenties disentangled from the crowd to Boris's left. One of them—a skeletal guy in a jean jacket—touched him on the shoulder. He turned and saw a hand with a joint in it. He almost took it, then changed his mind and said, "Thanks. And I don't think you should, either."

"What do you mean?" said Skeleton.

"There are too many cops around. Right here, behind the stage, I can see at least ten suspicious faces. You don't want to give them a chance to say this was a gathering of dopes."

"Yeah?" Skeleton's friend had close-cropped hair as black as his bomber jacket. "Well, however many cops you've found, I've just found another one."

Boris stared at him. He was clearly the leader of the pack.

"Okay, buddy, eleven, whatever. Just take it somewhere else, will you?"

"Tell me, *buddy*, how come you don't ask me where I found another cop? I saw you on TV the other day. You're now a city face, giving interviews on television. A big shot. The son of General Bulic."

"Listen, man, I don't know what your problem is, but take it home, okay?"

"This *is* my home, you piece of shit! Your father and his imbeciles sent my brother to war. What are you even doing here? Bulic is not a Serbian name!"

Boris could smell the beer on the man's breath as he and Skeleton and the two others crowded in on him. Then a blow caught the corner of his left eye and his vision blurred. His ear started ringing. A punch to his kidneys followed. Boris swung and missed, and the skinhead hit him in the stomach, winding him. He tried to protect his head with his hands and received several more punches to his ribs. Each hit was like a scream with no mouth. He heard someone yelling for them to stop but the blows kept coming. He tried to grab hold of something—anything—and felt someone's hand. He opened his eyes: Sara, her face red, yelling at his attackers.

Skeleton was on the ground, gasping, Johnny standing above him. A man in a striped shirt tried to kick Johnny, but his own nose exploded into a bloody flower. Boris heard the cracking of the bone. The man yelled, stumbled backwards and fell across a plastic chair. Johnny shook off the pain from his fist. The skinhead and the fourth man—a short gorilla—circled, trying to find a way to attack him from different angles. The crowd around them suddenly opened and the heavy boot of Johnny's drummer clobbered Gorilla's balls.

Several of the artists had come out of the bookstore with drinks in their hands. One of them, small and fat and wobbly on his legs, yelled, "That's right: screw the war! War is a collective effort, and therefore communism. We prefer man to man."

Some of the bystanders laughed, and Johnny dropped his hands, stepping back.

Then Sara yelled, and Boris saw a knife in the skinhead's hand. The crowd pushed back, widening the circle. Johnny grabbed a chair. His drummer was faster: his kick at the man's knee was enough to send him down. Johnny stood on the knife.

THE CAB. *September 29, 1992*

Boris spent his days following the same routine: he would get up around ten, go out for some pastries and an espresso, take a long walk through the centre of Belgrade, come home, improvise a lunch, and then sit and read. In the evening, he would turn on the television or sometimes drop by the small video store down the street, rent a movie, and watch it over a plate of cold cuts. Afterwards he would read some more until he was so tired his eyes started to itch. Only then would he go to bed.

In the days of strained reflection that followed the fight on the square, Boris came to realize that his routine was much like his father's had been: reading, watching TV, seeking out political news. There was a masochism in that: everywhere he turned, new people were coming to power. Not only in politically charged positions but in cultural institutions also. The publishing industry, media, theatres, even libraries. The regime had seeped into all the pores of public life and now was fortifying its posts. The process seemed based on negative selection—the worse the people were at the actual job, the better. Or perhaps it was Boris who had changed. To so many people around him the news sounded like a heroic symphony—maybe only he was out of key.

His mother always called in the early evening to check up on him. Somehow she had heard about the fight and she had apparently made a few calls. A man who presented himself as a police inspector came by one day to speak to Boris—who listened to him, then refused to pursue it. His mother would slip something in about his father when they talked—he hated Boris Yeltsin with a passion, his leg hurt again, he got a pocket watch from his party for his birthday—but Boris never rose to the bait. He knew enough about his father—he had seen him interviewed on the evening news, telling the world that he passionately supported the army intervention in Bosnia and Croatia against the separatist forces.

After the incident in the Square of the Republic, Boris had become cautious. His mother had asked him if he wanted a gun, but he knew where the question had come from and laughed it off. He took his long walks every day but kept changing his route. He had his morning espresso always in a different café, always sitting in a corner. Instead of making him feel safer, this hiding game—suggested by the policeman his mother had sent—turned him into an exile in his hometown.

Laughter did not work anymore, his food tasted like plastic, his cigarettes stank. There was a tension in him that brought a new intensity to his lovemaking, but his mood would sink surprisingly fast after an orgasm. His lovers seemed to like this new side of him. It felt like stealing pleasure from a well that would run dry someday. But in the middle of the night, Boris was empty, empty.

He had a few women around him who were occasional lovers. One was a doctor, two were art history students, and two others were journalists. All of them had their men: the doctor was married, and the rest had boyfriends. So there was no pressure. Everything was just for pleasure, and Boris made sure it stayed that way. When Nena, a tall, blond cello player in the symphony, started bringing food to his rented apartment close to Saint Marcus's Church, quietly arranging things so that she would have to stay the night, he broke up with her.

He tried to pretend to himself that this had nothing to do with Sara.

One Friday evening, some months before the protest, Boris encountered her in Knez Mihailova Street. Johnny was on tour, and she had come out for a stroll and to buy some books. The air was mild, the streets were full, and Boris wanted to find an excuse to stay out longer instead of going home to finish the text for a catalogue he was working on. Sara did not seem to be in a hurry, either, so Boris invited her for a drink. They went into a restaurant on a side street, and after a couple of drinks she said she was hungry, so they ordered food. He talked graphic novels; she told him anecdotes about famous people she had interviewed. They laughed a lot. After dinner, Boris walked her home. In front of the building Sara invited him upstairs for coffee. It all seemed perfectly normal—a good, strong coffee was something he really needed if he wanted to do his homework that night. They went upstairs, and the coffee was followed by another drink, and another, and at three in the morning Boris called a cab. He got up to leave, and they stood by the door—his hand already on the doorknob— when he saw something different in Sara's eyes, something that hadn't ever been there before, and he leaned towards her. They kissed, his hand still on the doorknob, her hands limp and still. The intercom rang: the cab had arrived. Boris ran down the stairs.

Johnny's tour lasted for three more weeks, but he didn't seek her out. Neither of them ever mentioned that night again. Neither of them knew what that kiss meant.

Many times since then, Boris asked himself if he should have cancelled his cab. Every time he did, he reminded himself that she could have, but didn't.

SHRINKING. *October 12, 1992*

"It feels somehow grey," Johnny said. "Everything is totally grey to me now."

Johnny's rented apartment was on the fifth floor of an old building across from the Belgrade Zoo. From the armchair where Boris sat, he could see the Danube in the distance, glowing under the last rays of daylight. The wind was picking up and the large chestnut tree, whose highest branches reached Johnny's windows, was getting balder with each new gust.

"It's strange. You're a musician and your colour perception has changed," Boris said. "I'm into visuals and to me the sound has gone. Everything is muted now. I miss majors: laughter, sex, flirting, joy, smiles, hugging. Everything I hear is in a minor key—sad stuff, ballads."

Johnny went to the kitchen to get some more ice for their whisky. "When was the last time you heard a good joke?" he yelled back.

Boris tried to remember. Before he could come up with the answer, Johnny returned with a toy bucket full of ice cubes with a pink plastic shovel stuck inside. "I'm seriously thinking that there must have been a date when the jokes died," he said.

"That's a good title. You should write it down."

"I did."

"Is laughter just inappropriate now?"

Johnny looked at the pale line of scar on his right hand. "Well, we are all becoming more brutal."

"I could do you a new poster," Boris said. " 'Johnny in concert: He will rock you, he will roll you, he will make you scream.' And below, in fine print: 'In pain.' "

They laughed.

The intercom buzzed. Johnny went to the front door, picked up the handset, listened for a second, and said, "Boris is here too." He pressed the button, turned the key in the lock, and returned to his seat. When Sara entered she hung up her umbrella, removed her black leather cap and shook her hair loose. Unbuttoning her jacket, she smiled at Boris. Her cheeks were slightly coloured from the wind, and her lips shiny with protective gloss. She was an inch taller than Boris in her high-heeled boots and had to bend a little when he stood up to hug her. She kissed him quickly on the lips and then touched the scar above his left eyebrow. "It hurts only when you laugh, right?"

"No, only when it's not kissed."

"Hey, what about me?" Johnny protested.

Sara sat on the armrest next to Johnny and said, "Guys, give me a drink. I want to celebrate."

"Celebrate what?" Boris asked, fumbling with an ice cube he had just caught with the pink shovel.

"I've just been fired."

Boris dropped the ice cube on the floor.

"Why?" Johnny asked.

"Officially, they say they are restructuring the cultural section of the evening news because of the war. Unofficially, they are cleaning up. They kicked a whole group of us out. Eleven from our department. We still don't know what's happening in the other sections. We've all spoken publicly against Milosevic at one time or another."

"You could sue them," Boris offered.

"Yes, and we will, but we don't stand a chance. They don't want to make martyrs of us so we're only 'suspended'— we'll all continue to receive our salaries until further notice. No one will understand what our problem is if they pay us every month." Sara went to the cupboard and took out a shot glass and a bottle of brandy, poured a drink for herself and returned to the armrest. Johnny patted her hand.

"Good for you," he said.

She took a swig. "It is, in a way."

He got up to change the disc in the player. Boris looked at Sara, head down, playing with her watch. Her lips curved up naturally, so that even when she was upset she looked as if she were smiling. Her heavy hair, almost black, framed her face tightly, making it appear narrower than it was.

"Why don't you write for a magazine?" Boris said. "You do terrific interviews—that always sells."

"Everyone is taking sides, Boris. Can you think of a single independent magazine that has lasted more than a month? You know that as well as I do—how many galleries would even think of exhibiting the project your group is doing? Two? One? Your space is shrinking. So is mine. Independence is expensive."

One gallery, only. And even that one only because its owner was the brother of one of the artists from Boris's group. The soundtrack of their lives: sad stuff, ballads. Their movie: grey frames in slow motion.

A gust of wind carried in the scream of some small animal caged across the street.

Johnny shook his head. "We can't play in Slovenia now, or Croatia, or Bosnia. Half of my audience is in Croatia. The other half, here, is worried. They don't have time for music."

They all froze in their thoughts, leaving Van Morrison to fill the void.

"Do you have any plans?" Boris asked Sara.

She stopped fiddling with her watch and looked him in the eyes. "Are you worried about me?"

"No," he said. "It's just so sudden. I don't know what I would do if I were you. I've never worked full-time so I don't know how it feels . . ."

Sara smiled. "I'm furious at them. And I will fight the idiots. You know me that much. But some of us who were suspended today are not that good. That's another trick they use, to mix it up a little, to cover their tracks. There are only maybe four of us who have a chance to get our jobs back. Even if they lose, they still win. It will last for months and even if they have to take the four of us back, it's still not that bad. They will have eliminated seven people."

She took another swig from her glass. This time her shoulders stayed level.

"Perhaps I'll put on a miniskirt and high heels and go to the office from time to time. That's the language they understand. That will give them some sleepless nights."

PAYBACK TIME. *November 5, 1992*

November started with cold rain. The northern wind, sliding down the Danube, occasionally added sleet to the mix.

Boris's exhibition had turned into a non-event. The crowd at the opening were mostly artists who all knew one another. The media scribbled down a few notes about it and that was that.

The book he was reading now was Charles Bukowski's *Erections, Ejaculations, Exhibitions and General Tales of Ordinary Madness.* He had brought it with him from Amsterdam the previous summer. He liked Bukowski but had bought this particular book because its title summarized the feeling he had that summer—and throughout this war, for that matter.

To finance the trip he'd sold a painting—he'd decided that he needed to remove himself from the overheated political noise. He chose Amsterdam because he knew the city, and it had always been good to him. But on the first day of his stay, he ran into two of his colleagues from Fine Arts and realized they both had emigrated—they were talking about how to find a job in welding or picking tulips. From their perspective, every sane person should leave Belgrade immediately. After parting with them, he went back to his hostel and opened his backpack. Two shirts, three pairs of underwear, two pairs of socks, sandals, three T-shirts, a sweater, a pack of condoms, five painkillers, and a bar of milk chocolate. Definitely not enough painkillers to emigrate. Bukowski's book was all he brought back.

Now he was reading it again because he needed a dose of reality. Life inside its covers was full of stench and love and passion and oblivion and madness. It soothed him. There was so much hypocrisy outside, so much distortion, he found it good to get down to the basics. Screw the high philosophy. His other antidote was Van Morrison. Boris played mostly *Poetic Champions Compose*, especially the instrumentals. He loved that album so much he bought a copy for Johnny so he could listen to it when he went to Johnny's place. Which was usually every day, but not now. Johnny was in Novi Sad recording with some local musicians and Sara was visiting distant cousins in Macedonia.

Boris looked at the absurdly large wall clock hanging above his desk. It was almost eleven and he put the book down and zapped through several channels trying to find a movie. Instead, he stumbled upon news on a satellite channel. Flashing images of Earth exchanged places with pictures from big cities of the world. The anchor was a prototype, probably a legend in German or Swiss journalism. Boris did not speak German, so he muted the box and reached for an ashtray and the notebook that lay next to it. Before he could light a cigarette, the telephone rang.

"Are you asleep?"

"No. Where are you?"

"Are you alone?" There was urgency in Johnny's voice.

"I am. Why?"

"Not over the phone. I'm back in Belgrade. We need to talk."

"Come over."

"I'll be there in twenty minutes, okay?"

Johnny hung up, and Boris put his small red phone back on the hook. He went to the kitchen and opened the window. He took out a few eggs, some cheese, and the remains of assorted salamis he found in the fridge behind the milk and set them on the counter. He put the frying pan on the stove and turned on the burner, then started mixing everything he had found in a bowl. When the oil in the pan started smoking, he emptied the bowl into it and let it fry for a minute or two. He removed the pan from the stove and set the table for two.

He opened the door to the small balcony and went outside, propping the door open to allow the fumes out. The street below was almost deserted. That was another thing that had changed with the coming of war. Normally, Belgrade was alive at any time of night, except maybe around four in the morning, when the night owls would be withdrawing before the skunks of day. A cab stopped below him and Johnny got out.

"I thought you were supposed to be in Novi Sad," Boris said, taking Johnny's old, long coat.

"I thought so, too. But people have other plans for me."

"What people?"

Johnny looked at him, not yet ready to talk.

"All right, let's eat. I made a little something. Wine?"

"Anything to warm up, it's biting outside."

As Johnny sat down at the kitchen table, Boris poured some red wine into the water glasses he'd grabbed from the sink. Johnny took a long gulp and Boris refilled his glass.

Johnny stared at his plate, then pushed it away. "You eat, I'll keep you company."

"What's going on?"

"Well, it seems that we pissed someone off with our concert in the square."

"I'm sure we did," Boris said, chewing on his omelette.

"Yeah, but it's payback time. At least for me."

Boris reached for his glass.

"Last night we worked 'til two in the studio. It was good so we stayed a little longer to celebrate. When I got back to my hotel, there was a message for me. It said, 'Call Mr. Stosic, extension 517, whenever you get back to your room.' It was past three in the morning and I don't know anyone by that name so I ignored it and got ready for bed. The telephone rang. I was rude, but the guy cut me off—he was from State Security, he said. He suggested that I meet him in the morning in the hotel restaurant. At first I thought he was pulling my leg but then I realized that the guy knew I'd just returned to my room so he could have indeed been a cop.

"This morning, I'm downstairs having my breakfast, and the guy comes to my table and sits with me. He doesn't look anything like a cop. He was our age, jeans, leather, all that. Big shoulders. Snake eyes. He orders a coffee and gets right down to business."

"Where was the good cop?" Boris said.

"This guy was both. You know—a little hot, then a little cold, slaps you with his left hand, pets you with his right."

"What did he say?"

"That there is a war going on, and although Serbia is not part of it, we have to be ready to prevent it spilling over the border. So the military is doing exercises to keep people awake. All reservists are to take that seriously, and at the moment they are not. I am a symbol, he says, so popular and important, and he's here to tell me that for the good of Serbia I have to go to one of those exercises."

"What?"

"Yeah. He said the purpose of his visit was to warn me not to fool around when I get the call. He said that if I cooperated, they wouldn't use me for direct propaganda. You know, no pictures of Elvis in uniform, no haircut, nothing. But I am in deep shit no matter what. Because we both know that even if Elvis doesn't pose, selected journalists will be told that I am fulfilling my patriotic duties. And they will publish it. Otherwise, why am I so important as a symbol? And then I can go play at weddings and funerals. Or just funerals."

"What happens if you don't go?"

"I could end up in jail."

"For what?"

"He showed me pictures. You, me, and Sara smoking pot."

"No!"

"Yes."

"Where?"

"I'm not sure, but I think it was at a party last summer."

"The guy with the pool?"

"Probably."

"I didn't know he was a snitch. Jesus, Johnny, I took you there."

They remained silent for a while, Johnny spinning his glass slowly, Boris smoking.

Boris sighed.

Johnny continued to spin his glass without looking up.

"I'll talk to the General," Boris said.

VANILLA. *November 9, 1992*

His mother was chirpy as she announced that she'd serve coffee in the living room.

The living room, and not his study? Of course: generals negotiate on no man's land. Boris put down the book he was holding and said, "Thanks, Mom, I'll be right there."

"You know he can't stand waiting," she whispered, her back keeping the sound of her voice from spilling into the hall.

Boris sighed and stood up, glancing around. When he had arrived at the apartment half an hour earlier, his mother had ushered him here into his old room to wait. Entering, he had expected an avalanche of barbed memories, but it didn't come. The space looked smaller. As soon as he had moved out, they had turned it into a guest room. Not that they ever had any guests.

He followed his mother down the hall. The General was sitting in his usual chair, and though the newspaper was open on the table in front of him, Boris knew that he was not reading. The glasses sitting low on his father's nose were just an excuse to hold his head in a position from which he could not see him entering.

"Hello, Father," Boris said.

"Hello, Boris."

It had been three and a half years since he'd seen his father, except on television. His hair was still black, aside from some grey in his sideburns and at his temples. There were two deep lines at the corners of his mouth that Boris didn't remember, but his grey eyes had the same edge as always in the same square, masculine face that Boris had hoped for when he had entered puberty, and didn't get.

Boris glanced at his mother. There was nothing new on her face—they met for coffee once or twice a month, always at her request, always in the same café—but it seemed that she had acquired some of her husband's aspect. He saw it only now, with the two of them next to each other: the same stiffness of their necks, their lips thinning with age and turning downward at the corners, their eyebrows somehow lighter and readier to lift.

It had taken her three days to soften up the old man enough for Boris's visit.

The coffee was bitter and strong, served in large cups, just the way the General liked it. Only Mother's cup was her usual small one. *Look, husband, even my coffee cup is smaller than yours.*

They each took a sip. There was no ashtray on the table. The General did not allow smoking in his home. It was like meeting an old love: the breakup was painful but time does its tricks, and you sit down over a coffee, hoping that everything will be like it used to be, but then she puts three cubes of sugar in her cup, the thing that always drove you crazy, and you start with, "So?", the word she hated with a passion.

"How is it going?" Boris asked.

The General looked at him over his glasses, then took them off, slowly, methodically, folded them and put them into a narrow leather sheath.

"Swell, as always," he finally responded. "You?"

"Not bad."

Mother pushed the plate with vanilla cookies she had baked towards them. "Boys," she said, "have some, they are still warm." Neither responded.

The scent of vanilla filled the room.

"Look," the General started, "this must be difficult for you, I can gather that much. And you are my son. I don't want to make it harder."

Had Mother prepared him? Did she know something? From whom? Will this be that easy?

"The times are good for bad people, and awful for everyone who has some brains." The General sighed. "In such times, we have to help one another, otherwise we are immoral. I think it is great that you are here. I salute that." He allowed himself a smile.

"Thanks," Boris said.

Dear Mom. Dear, dear Mom. He hadn't told her why he wanted to talk to the General, but perhaps she had talked to Sara, or even Johnny—who knows?

"Your mother told me about that attack on you. Those men must have been on drugs, or insane. In any case, you should put it behind you."

"I already have."

"Good."

"His new exhibition has just opened," Boris's mother said.

"Mother—"

"No, no, she's right," his father interrupted. "I should go see it. It's been too long since I saw any of your works. There are no silly pictures of us this time, I hope?" His father's face actually softened into another smile.

"No," Boris said, "these are sculptures."

"Good."

All three of them sipped their coffee.

"Have you heard that your old friend Maestro, the theatre director—?"

"Yes, I know who—"

"He became a secretary in our party."

Boris raised his eyebrows.

"Precisely," said his father. "I had the same reaction. I mean, he's dedicated to our cause, that's fine, but he doesn't have any sort of political experience."

Why was the General telling him this?

"Many people do not realize that we have much more power than it seems from the outside. Milosevic and his party are running the show, but our party was founded by his wife, and she has huge influence on her husband." The General's tone was content. He ran his fingers through his hair. "We don't hold too many important positions in the current power structure, but it suits us—most of us prefer to be guerrillas, as you know."

Guerrilla? He had been an army general.

61

Boris's father reached for the plate and took a cookie.

"We don't need propaganda, we need people who know how things are done. Some separatists in Bosnia and Croatia want to destroy our country, and we have to protect it. It is a very simple, very clear situation."

Boris knew his father enough not to interrupt him. Instead, he looked at the bookshelf behind the General, and it looked the same as always: the same set of lonely virginal books that will never know the pleasure of being held open. Except . . . there was no *Gulag* there now.

"What happened when the Fascists came to power in Spain?" The General raised his finger to underline his words. "All the leading intellectuals lined up against them. The international brigades. You learned about it at school. When Hitler signed the pact with the Yugoslav king, all our leading intellectuals took up arms. Poets went to the woods, painters, sculptors! Now there are hundreds of people volunteering to go to Bosnia and fight. People of all ages and backgrounds."

"Now, now," Mother said. "Don't get too excited, your gout will flare up."

The General looked at her, incredulous, then turned to Boris: "That's your mother—we are saving the country, and she doesn't want me to aggravate my gout."

In spite of his words, he reached out to pat her hand. Boris thought that he should remember that detail.

"I was very angry when your mother told me about that attack. But I have to tell you that you were in the wrong place, in my opinion. I don't understand those musicians. Against the war! Against what? Against the fight for freedom? They are blind. Their friends are somewhere in the mud losing limbs for their country, dying, but they don't want their guitars to get rusty—they have to play their music. It's pathetic." The General waved his hand, dismissing them all as hopeless. "And, of course, the criminals and lunatics and junkies came to give their support, and attacked you." He spread his arms wide: a perfectly logical explanation.

Boris suddenly felt tired. So this is how they had read his call: the black sheep wants to go blond again.

The General continued his monologue, but Boris stopped listening. He finished his coffee, waited for a pause long enough to insert an apology, then stood up.

At the door, he stopped, turned around, and said, "Father, thank you for this."

The General, standing by the table, smiled. "No problem, son."

Vanilla in the air. Sweet and bitter. Switter. Closing the door gently behind him.

The stairs.

The exit.

The street.

ONE SECOND AFTER. *December 9, 1992*

Outside the big window of the bookstore café on the Square of the Republic, people moved fast, driven by the northern wind. The majority of passersby were in dark coats, as if Boris was watching an old black-and-white movie.

"Where is he now, do you know?" he said.

Sara shook her head.

Johnny's gathering point was in a camp outside of town, on the highway to the south. He had called a few times during the first week, but now silence.

"It's my fault."

"Don't be ridiculous, Boris."

"No, it is, it really is. First I took you both to that stupid party where they spied on us. Then I was too stubborn to ask the only person who could do something for help."

"Let's just try to find him. I've heard all these stories."

"What stories?"

"That they say they are just doing a military exercise but then they smuggle some of the men across the border to fight."

Johnny understood now why everyone around him was drinking. When his brain was not bleary with drink, he needed no other enemy.

He was lying under a barren tree, covered with dry leaves. The mud caked on his uniform and his face made him invisible to anyone who did not know where to look. He was aware of the irony: he looked like a hardened soldier but only because he had tripped and fallen. How long ago, he was not sure. If he could only lie here for several months, it would be over.

He had taken a cab to the gathering spot. The man who drove it was Johnny's age, knew his music well and was delighted to have him in his car. His adulation soothed Johnny, and when he got out of that cab, he thought he was ready for their stupid military games.

The feeling kept him going for the first few days.

Everything was as they had promised: there were no photographers, no obvious propaganda being made, just serious-looking officers doing the drill. Not many people had been drafted, though, and the barracks were half empty.

Strange things started happening late in the evening of the eighth day, just as everyone expected to be released. A Jeep and a black car arrived at the camp after dinner and the officers disappeared from the cantina. An hour later, the men reported to their barracks, and their officers read the instructions for the next day. They were to perform an emergency exercise. In the case of a sudden attack from Croatia, reservists were to be transported to the area around the Danube as quickly as possible. That would be the aim of tomorrow's exercise—to clock the time needed. All reservists were expected to adhere to the emergency rules, which meant, among other things, that communication with the outside world was forbidden from that moment on. The lines from both public phones in the camp had been cut.

They were dismissed and went to bed immediately afterwards, but no one in Johnny's room fell asleep. In the dark someone said what everyone was thinking: "This might be it, brothers. They're lying to us—we'll end up in Bosnia." That's where the slaughter had moved to.

The next morning, they got up early, did some funny gymnastics, went to breakfast, and reported for weapons practice. They remained on the range until late afternoon. When they got back, they cleaned their weapons and packed their rucksacks. There was a break before dinner, but instead of using it to get some rest, most reservists stood around in groups, tense, smoking and discussing various options of running away. Dinner was at seven. Half an hour later, a siren sounded. The officers started yelling and everyone ran to their barracks, grabbed their bags and their weapons, and gathered before a line of trucks that had entered the yard. Ten minutes later, Johnny was sitting on a wooden bench in the back of a truck, swaying and bumping as the small convoy turned off the main highway onto a poorly lit local road. But they did drive northwest, towards Croatia, where a ceasefire had held for most of a year. Those near the tailgate kept peeking out from under the tarpaulin, reading out the names of the towns they passed: Indjija, Karlovci, Palanka, Deronje.

"They can't do that to us, send us to Croatia," the man who sat next to Johnny said.

"Why not?" said another. "We're already conscripted. If we run now it would be deserting and we'd end up in front of a military court."

"Yes, but we're not at war with Croatia. We're only sending weapons to the Serbs who live there so they can defend themselves. If someone saw us, Milosevic would have to admit Serbia was taking part, and it would mean huge troubles for him."

"Well, my ass tells me that nobody will see us, comrades," said the company joker. "If they continue driving us across fields like this, I will come off this truck walking like John Wayne."

Nervous laughter.

Johnny kept silent. His gut was telling him to jump off

the truck the next time it stopped, but his brain kept reassuring him—there was no way they were being driven to the front. The night was now silent and the villages they passed through were asleep. Some of the soldiers around him laid their blankets on the wooden floor of the truck and tried to nap. Johnny wadded his blanket against the metal bars behind his back and closed his eyes. He drifted in and out of sleep, his dreams short and feverish.

"Apatin," said someone. "Surely we're almost there, wherever it is." The trucks kept driving.

"We are entering the swamps," said a harsh voice several minutes later, as if commenting a football match on the radio. A short while later, the truck stopped.

"Fuck," said the same harsh voice again.

"What?"

"Boats are waiting for us. Croatia is on the other side."

A second later the tarpaulin at the back of the truck was yanked aside. Three men stood looking up at them. One of them had a few stars on his shoulders.

"Good evening, soldiers," he said. "I am Captain Pap. You might be asking yourselves what is going on. In short: you are needed here, so we brought you here. We won't stay long, only until the local Serbs get organized and secure the area. That's the good news. As usual, there is more bad news than good. First, we do not exist here. You cannot tell anyone where you are. Not now, not ever. Second, we don't start anything—whether we fight does not depend on us but on the madmen on the other side, and there are plenty of them. Third, I am your commander. Wake up now, but stay silent, and keep your heads low. We are about to cross the river. You will get ammunition on the other side and then we will continue on foot for several miles. No talking until I tell you. No lighters or cigarettes. We are entering the war zone and joking around could cost you your life. All clear? Good. We'll head out in five minutes."

The canvas fell, cutting off a piece of night and leaving it inside.

It was half past four when they got to their camp, which consisted of a group of tents in a glade deep in the forest on the Croatian side of the Danube. Pap ordered several of them to stand guard and sent the rest to sleep. Like the others, Johnny fell asleep in his uniform.

He did not know how long he'd been out when someone shook his shoulder, but judging by the weight of his eyelids, it was probably no more than a couple of hours. In silence, they were led out of the camp. Johnny could hear the distant crowing of roosters. Two hours later, they came to a small clearing around a shack and Pap gave them the at-ease signal. Most of them sat down under the trees, laid their equipment on the ground, and tried to get some more sleep. Pap and the two sergeants who had joined them went into the shack and stayed there.

Johnny had an idea where they were. When he was in high school, he had played at a festival where he met a girl with whom he'd had a brief long-distance relationship. She lived in Beli Manastir, a small town that had to be nearby. That meant they were in a pocket close to the Hungarian border. He tried to remember if he had heard something about the fighting in this area. Perhaps it was true what Pap had said, that they were here only for security.

He found a spot at the edge of the clearing, behind a birch tree, and soon fell asleep again.

He woke up around noon to the cawing of a crow in the tree above him. As soon as he moved it flew away. He tried to remember where he was, and why, and found a wobbly answer for the first question only. Some of his platoon were awake, sitting around in small groups. There were new people among them, all dressed in black uniforms, all cleanly shaven with military haircuts, and Kalashnikovs. Some special unit. Then he noticed that some of them wore sneakers. Some had bandanas. Paramilitaries?

Johnny got up, stretched, brushed the leaves off his uniform, and went to the shack. He knocked.

"Come in!" barked a voice from behind the door.

Pap was sitting at the table in the corner. One of the sergeants was making coffee on a small burner, and the other was cleaning his gun. A fourth man was sitting with Pap at the table. He wore battle fatigues and had black aviator sunglasses on the top of his head. He looked vaguely familiar.

"Hello, gentlemen," Johnny said. One of the sergeants nodded in his direction.

"I wanted to talk to you, Captain," Johnny said to Pap.

"What about?"

"It's private."

"There is not much privacy in war, I'm afraid," Pap said.

"I am—"

"I know who you are."

Johnny remained silent.

"You are here by mistake. Or, wait, perhaps we were not allowed to bring you here?" Pap waited for Johnny to nod, and when he did not, the captain's face relaxed slightly. "Would you like a coffee, Johnny? Come, join us."

Pap pushed a chair over with his boot, and Johnny took it. He waited to be introduced, but Pap had no such intention. A sergeant brought the coffee to their table and poured it into three metal cups. There was a long silence.

"I've seen a few new people outside," Johnny said.

"Locals. We're here to help them."

Silence.

"What's the time, artist?" Pap said.

"I don't have a watch, Captain."

"Forgot it at home when you went to war. I see."

"I never went to war."

"Don't get entangled in nuances. The war came to you, as it did to us. It always does. So, if I order you to commence firing at sixteen hundred, when will you start shooting, artist?"

"One second after someone with a watch."

One of the sergeants laughed. The captain said, "Boys, leave us alone," and they did, the door slamming behind them. The other man stayed where he was.

"So, what is your problem, then?"

"Well," Johnny said, "I was drafted for the exercise. The draft said five days. It didn't say anything about a week and there was definitely nothing about the war. In which, by the way, Serbia is not taking part. I mean—wouldn't it be dangerous if someone from the foreign media were to learn about us being here?"

Pap looked straight into Johnny's eyes, but Johnny was accustomed to people looking at him. He also knew that avoiding the captain's sniper stare would mean submission. Not to this man. His basic strategy had been to get some sense of whoever was running this show, and then get away from here as fast as he could. There was not much left of his plan.

"Ah," the captain finally said, "you got me there. I told you to avoid nuances but they are important, of course. It's true that Serbia is not at war with anyone. But you are not in the Serbian army, are you? We are the Yugoslav People's Army and this is still Yugoslavia until the politicians decide it's not. We can have our exercises wherever we please, including the combat zone. And we can exercise with live ammunition to our heart's content. So we're legit here. Regarding the foreigners, who cares what they think? It's our country that's falling apart, not theirs."

Johnny waited a few seconds for him to go on, and when he didn't, he said, "There were rather large protests against the war in Belgrade just recently. I took part in them. Am I being punished for that?"

The third man got up. "I'll be back later, Captain," he said, "after you put the babies to sleep."

Johnny stared after him as he left.

Pap took a notebook out of his leather officer bag. "It's good that you didn't get into an argument with him."

Johnny felt a change in Pap's tone.

"His face seemed familiar."

"To you, Interpol, and several tens of dead men."

"Ah," Johnny said. "The Candyman."

"The men outside, they are his private army. They call themselves the Black Lions. Actually, they seem to be the advance guard. He's just told me they have around sixty more fighters coming tomorrow and three tanks. They've got Uzis, they've got Magnums, and they have a few cannons available. They've got more than I do."

"What do you think my chances are of getting out of here?" Johnny said.

"Right now, none. Stay put and keep a low profile. This is apparently getting out of control—that's what the Candyman's arrival means. Our secret service has employed criminals for decades, and now it's payback time. They must have opened the prisons and let the worst out."

Johnny looked at him. Was he afraid of the gangster?

"Would you like a drink?" Pap asked.

"Why not?"

The captain poured two shots and pushed one towards Johnny, then raised his, waiting for Johnny to do the same.

"Cheers," he said, "and may we survive this shit."

Johnny was suddenly aware of birdsong outside the cabin walls. It was not pleasant, sounding more like short screams, but anything was better than gunshots.

"Make no mistake, artist: I, too, don't want to be here. I know, I am a professional soldier, I chose this uniform, but those were different times: brotherhood and unity. Then this started. My colleagues chose their sides fast. I am where I am because my parents were Serbs. There is no choice in that."

Johnny drank a little from his glass. The brandy was strong and sharp, probably made that same year. The captain lit a cigarette and inhaled deeply.

"I once fucked a girl in Zagreb when I was serving there. She was ugly but she was a nymphomaniac so what the hell. Ideal for a soldier. We were next to a yard gate and when she bent over, I could see a tattoo on her lower back. The letters were old German, hard to read. Small print, three lines. Had someone passed by, he would have seen us, screwing like dogs at the gate, but it still took me an hour to come. Well, maybe I had a cheap watch, but it was the best fuck of my life. You know why it took me that long? Because I kept trying to read the tattoo. See? At first, I thought it was so kind of her to have something for people to read while they were fucking her. Years later I realized it was her neat little trick to squeeze the best out of her riders. How is that related to this now? This uniform on us, my friend, is the tattoo on our asses. Think about it. Lay low, and stay low."

Johnny's hand was already on the latch when Pap waved at him to wait. He opened a drawer in the desk, pulled out a watch, and threw it to him. "Here. You never know. Keep it, I have more here. They are a gift from the Candyman for our boys."

Johnny looked at the watch. It was a Rolex. He looked at Pap.

"No blood on them. They are from a truck that was parked on the wrong side of the road somewhere in Austria, I'm told."

Johnny went outside to sit under his birch tree again. Not noticing a root hidden in the leaves, he tripped over it and fell. He cursed, rolled over, and decided to stay where he was. He looked at the sky. It was low and claustrophobic.

The flatlands in the distance were his country, which he and others like him wanted to keep together, but he felt only coldness coming from there. He didn't want to die fighting for this place.

He tried to block the wisps of quiet conversation drifting towards him. He thought of Sara . . . She was probably trying to find him, trying to do something about his being here. And Boris—he must be accusing himself now, as he always did. He was desperate when he returned from meeting his father. But he'd be there for Sara—she could count on him.

After a while, the wind seemed to carry all the sound away. And then, just as his eyes were closing, he was certain he could actually hear the silence. It was dark, and gentle, and it fell in flakes, like black snow. A thought accompanied him into the blackness: my whole world is freezing now.

NOTHING GOING ON. *December 13, 1992*

More people joined the camp, some of them in civilian clothes and without any visible arms, some of them apparently Black Lions. They moved to an abandoned socks factory, which—in spite of the broken windows and the stink of bird droppings—gave them much better protection than the few tents they'd had in the clearing. Someone had even fixed the water so they could use the showers and toilets, though there was no electricity.

Johnny was grateful when Pap gave him a spare notebook and a pencil. He started jotting down fragments of conversation, a verse here and there, some notes. He'd had music in his head as far back as he could remember. It was fully orchestrated and grandiose when he was happy, edgy and fragmented when he felt bad. Now all he heard was the echo of his shredded thoughts. Perhaps it was time to write a book. He had wanted to write one for the past—how long? Six years? Eight? At first he thought that maybe he would write a memoir but realized that too much had happened to him—his memories were overgrown and dense, like jungle. Once, during a dinner party, he had sat next to a well-known writer and confessed his desire. "Of course you want to write a book," the writer said. "And I dream of making a record. We all want to jump out of our skins, but in the end only a few do it."

Definitely, this was a great time to jump out of his skin. The only good thing about sitting here in the backwoods was that the notion of war had thinned out. Weapons and uniforms, trucks and orders—yes, all that, but other things too: listening to the wind and the murmur of dry leaves, watching the endless movie of the clouds, engaging in the small talk, the crude jokes, or escaping it all in his thoughts. How long had it been? Johnny had to count the days. More than a week for sure. Ten days? Eleven? It was December.

The drizzle that had come in short intervals all morning stopped and an easterly wind picked up. When the sun appeared, people crawled out from the factory to warm their bones.

Johnny stayed inside, writing. The even rhythm of his hand and the slow dripping of thoughts lulled him to sleep.

He woke up with a strong erection. He could not recall anything from his dreams and the stubbornness in his crotch surprised him. His first thought, almost automatic, was that he had dreamt of fucking with Sara, but there was no way of being certain about it.

He used to be good at remembering his dreams. Several times, the scenes he had dreamt were so powerful that he felt compelled to write songs about them. There had been a dream behind "Angel of Revenge." In that one, a woman with beautiful lips—who was his lover, his mother, his sister, and himself—told him of the injustice done to her by a group of soldiers guarding the gate to her house. He had felt terrible anger, and had killed them all with his bare hands. When he was finished with the last one, she came over to him, touched his eyebrow, raising it, and said, "I am your destiny now. You can fuck me."

But he hadn't been able to remember his dreams since they'd brought him here—as if the contrast between the world of dreams and the reality around him was so big that it evaporated the fine tissue. As if the dreams needed a softer landing than he could afford them now.

He was headed towards the bathroom when some soldiers came back in talking loudly.

"Something is going on outside," one of them said. "About thirty people in brand-new fatigues arrived with several Jeeps, one with a heavy machine gun mounted on it. The Candyman got out of that one and went to see the captain. They're distributing food outside. Go while there's still good stuff."

Johnny went outside and stood in line. Someone ahead of

him said that an order had been given to get ready to move after sunset.

"Finally, some action," said one of the paramilitaries, a broad-shouldered man in his mid-twenties who sat next to Johnny after they got their food. He wore a red bandana and green sunglasses and introduced himself as Black.

"Johnny, how come you're with us?" Black asked.

"I was brought here with the others," Johnny said, "like cattle, on a truck."

"Thought so. I watched the concert in the square."

Johnny turned to him. "Then how come you're here?"

Black didn't answer.

The rain started suddenly as if it had been ordered to do so. The two of them moved farther back under the bush and continued to cut off and chew on pieces of smoked meat.

"Black," Johnny said after a while, "have you already—?"

"Been in combat? Yeah. Good stuff, if you're the right man. Like nothing else. I personally think I'm a better man because of it. When it starts, you are transparent to yourself. You have nothing to lean on, except a bullet. It clears your head."

"But shooting at other people . . ."

"There's not much to it. Nothing personal. You and the guy who's shooting at you—you are just men at work."

He looked at Johnny, pursed his lips. "If you mean what you say in your songs, you should be okay."

Johnny thought for a while. "I'm not sure about one B-side."

Black laughed.

"Seriously, how did you get here?" Johnny asked.

"I volunteered. I was a graphic designer in Belgrade. My grandfather, on my mother's side, was from this area. As a kid, I used to spend my summers here. When this mess started, I thought, Who gives you the right to fuck with my childhood? So I decided to come. My old man is a retired soldier. He tried to keep me from doing this but when he realized I was serious, he said, 'Find the most experienced commander.' I asked around, and heard that the Candyman was gathering his troops. Only two other Lions besides me have never been in jail."

He swallowed the last bite and folded his knife.

One of the paramilitaries whistled and Black stood up. As he left he said, "One more thing, Johnny: after battle, don't look around too much."

The rain stopped as suddenly as it had started and the diffuse light withdrew before the falling darkness. The place where Johnny was sitting was dry and there was no one close to him, which suited him fine. He thought about that last sentence of Black's, but couldn't find any key to it, and gave up. He watched the glimmering lights in the scattered houses in the distance. Do those people know we are this close? he thought. If they do, do they feel protected or are they shivering now?

For a second he thought of writing a letter to Sara. What would he say? He felt like Jonah, only the animal that swallowed him was not a whale but a wild black dog, full of fleas, with rabies foaming out of his snout and blood in his eyes. The only good thing was that the dog already had him in its intestines and wasn't crawling around his house waiting to kill.

What would happen if he sneaked through the woods, covered in mud and darkness, and just deserted? He looked around. Quietly, the paramilitaries had taken up posts around the perimeter of the camp. Probably because they were the only group here with combat experience. Probably not in order to prevent strange ideas.

The two sergeants were crisscrossing the clearing, quietly ordering the conscripts to gather in the middle. Johnny got up and joined them.

The captain was concise: "There is a village three miles away. The Croats are the majority there and they are terrorizing the few remaining local Serbs, mostly old folks. It used to be just threats and extortion, but the situation has suddenly worsened—an old man was dragged out of his home and his throat was cut. They left him lying in his yard, as a warning. They want all the Serbs to leave. Our sources in the village claim that the Croats have planned further actions for tonight. Our enemy is not a regular army—we are the only regular army in this area. Our duty is to protect those civilians. The enemy wear black uniforms and are well armed with modern weapons. They number about thirty-five to forty people, some of whom are suspected to be mercenaries with significant combat experience. The Lions will attack the village from the east and we will close the exit on the other side to cut the enemy off. Our task is to expel the thugs from the village, arrest as many of them as possible, and eliminate those who resist. Don't shoot them if they surrender, but do not risk your lives. Make sure you see their arms high.

"The attack will start at twenty-one hundred.

"One more thing: you are fighting for your country. You gave your oath to protect it. Now is the time. Fifty years ago, Croatia took Hitler's side. Their blackshirts are butchering again. Don't expect any mercy from them because you won't get any. Imagine that your grandparents are in that village, waiting for their throats to be cut tonight. You are their only hope. Fight well and good luck, soldiers!"

In the past several days Sara's face had become thinner and sharper. Her skin, always so radiant, had lost its glow. She used her makeup well, but Boris saw shadows beneath her eyes and her lips were tightly pressed together. She always tilted her head when she was talking, and now the light of the sconce above her made shadows move on her face like storm clouds. "What if they make him shoot people, Boris?"

"Sara, I am doing everything I can, really. I told you— the only answer I could come up with is that he was transferred to some unit on the border with Croatia."

"I could go there with a TV crew, pretending that I'm doing a story . . ."

"And then what? No, that's ridiculous. Nothing is going on in Croatia now. Besides, I'm sure he'll find a way to let us know where he is. We can only wait."

It was a stupid thing to say, Boris knew. Even he did not know how to wait, or what to wait for.

Boris had found the right people through his mother and he had done everything to find Johnny. Almost all the traces of the conscript party had been destroyed except for a single link to a shadowy unit rumoured to be under the

Candyman's command. And *that* he had no heart to tell her. His fucking fault.

The night was wet and cold and smelled of unknown soil, of threatening trees, of strange animals. They approached the village from the west. The column of about a hundred people did not make much noise. The Black Lions were mostly ahead but another not so small group was at the back. A few hundred yards from the first houses, the men in front of Johnny stopped. The paramilitaries took the northern route around the village and the soldiers moved farther south. By Johnny's new Rolex it was twenty minutes to nine. His hands were cold and stiff. His gun was the same weight as his guitar. The houses before them were big and white with many large red tractors next to the stables and cars in the driveways. A rich village. Now.

The wind suddenly changed direction. Two dogs started barking fiercely and then several others joined in. A horse neighed in one of the stables.

It was twelve minutes to nine. Johnny hoped that nobody would come in his direction, that he wouldn't have to shoot at all. The leather strap on his gun was identical to the one on his Stratocaster, which Boris had given to him. *Sara, I'm fucking dying tonight, or killing someone, which is one and the same.* The wind changed direction again and the barking turned into a growl. A sergeant signalled to Johnny to stay put behind the second to the last house. He knelt in the wet grass, felt around him, and lay down. There was a wooden fence twenty yards in front of him and behind it one of the dogs continued to bark madly, not fooled by the sudden absence of the smell of strangers. Johnny's bowels howled so loudly he was glad for the dog. A light came on on the upper floor. A sheer curtain hung from a small window in the middle. ~~Boris~~ Johnny saw an old man inside. The dog was jumping at the fence. The old man had an empty look on his face, as if his only job was to urinate. Johnny's stomach was cold and he tried to find a better position. He put his gun on the ground and inched forward on his elbows. His left hand suddenly felt hot and Johnny pulled it back and squeezed it with his other hand, feeling blood on his fingers. There must have been some broken glass in the grass. He drew his hand closer to his eyes, hoping to be able to see the wound in the bit of light coming from the window, but the light flicked off. Just as Johnny reached into his pocket looking for something to stop the bleeding, the shooting started.

Sara watched Boris reaching into his pocket for something to stop the bleeding. Nothing. He grabbed the end of the tablecloth and pulled fast. It almost worked: only two glasses fell on the floor. "Shit!" he said. People turned to stare.

"Shit!" Sara said, squeezing her wrist with her hand. The cuts on her palm were not too deep but there were several of them.

"I'll fix it, hold still." Boris ripped a strip off the tablecloth and folded it into something that resembled a bandage and wrapped her palm with it. "Does it hurt much?"

"No," she said, checking to see if the blood had stained her dress, "it's just that everyone will say I was wasted."

"Who cares?"

"Maybe the glass was already cracked or something. I just squeezed and it went to pieces."

She had not wanted to come. The annual design awards show was always a bore and most people were there only to get drunk or to get laid, or both. But Boris insisted that it would do her good to go out and he invited her to accompany him. And so they went together. The party was at a villa surrounded by embassies. Its pool hadn't been filled with water for the past twenty years, so the organizers corralled guests into it and set the stage on the grass beyond. The prize night had been a low-key event for the past few years, but it was wartime now and people responded disproportionately to anything even remotely like fun. The number of guests crowded into the pool made for some rather intimate encounters. When a woman behind Sara started talking about the paramilitaries, and how—can you believe it?—even Johnny was with one such unit, actually, the worst of them all, the Candyman's team, Sara squeezed her glass hard. She did not want to repeat this preposterous lie to Boris. Because what else could it have been?

One early evening before the war had begun, when spring had already started kicking, Sara and Johnny had made love instead of going to a theatre premiere. Afterwards, lying naked, entangled, they listened to the traffic noise. After a while, Johnny went to his stereo to put some music on. Squatting by the shelf with the discs, his back turned to her, he said, "They are clogging the arteries."

"What?" Sara said.

"The politicians. They will take us to war, they don't care. It is clear they don't know how to run the country and they can't stay in power long. War is a great solution for them, perhaps the only chance they've got. But war doesn't mean only death and destruction. That happens on the front. What happens in the rear?" He pulled out a disc, put it on, and returned to bed. Satie floated above their heads.

Leaning on her elbow, Sara reached over him for her glass of wine. "What about the arteries?"

"Listen. Satie is flowing through the air, between the leaves of the chestnut tree and down the street, like clear water. What do you think will happen when the war starts? When fear pushes us all in different directions? There will be speed, and selfishness, and paralysis, and hatred. That slime will replace blood, and the gunk will make it impossible to take a step. The blood flow to the brain will become a trickle, there will be no strength in the muscles, no possibility of an erection. And then this system will stick a giant cock into our asses and screaming with joy as it fucks us will be an obligatory patriotic duty."

No, no, it wasn't possible at all. Not Johnny. Not her Johnny.

The cab was waiting outside. Boris helped Sara in and then eased himself into the backseat next to her. He gave the driver directions to her apartment.

Sara did not turn her head to him.

"Sara?"

He slowly put one arm around her shoulders and hugged her. She said, "I'm not crying, Boris. I'm just confused. And maybe afraid, I don't know."

Boris sighed. "I've talked to the people at the Canadian embassy, Sara. I'm getting out of here."

She turned to look into his eyes.

Johnny tried to look away but could not. The man's eyes and mouth were open—he seemed disconnected rather than dead. Johnny couldn't see any blood on his clothes and he thought for a second that maybe he had been frightened to death. Then he noticed the dark stain on the left side of his chest.

He got up from where he was crouching and headed for the house on the left where all the windows were lit. Its inhabitants, very likely the whole family, were out in the back yard talking to several soldiers from his unit. He got only a few steps before his intestines erupted with pain, forcing a yell from his throat. He bent over as if he had been hit and started throwing up. It lasted for an eternity. Finally, he felt someone kneel beside him and cup his forehead with a palm. It was a strong hand and though the touch was neither gentle nor friendly, Johnny felt better instantly. His breath slowly returned. He wiped his mouth with his sleeve and muttered, "I'm okay." He stood up and found a young woman in front of him, wearing a bulky sweater and jeans tucked into leather boots.

"You need some water," she said. "Come with me."

Following her into the yard, Johnny heard one of the villagers say, "Give him a shot of brandy, Mira."

In the house, Mira showed him to a chair in the living room and went to the kitchen. The walls were white and bare, the furniture dark and shiny, the gun on the coffee table in front of him small enough to be hidden up a sleeve.

She returned with a pitcher and a glass. "Sip it slowly," she said, putting them on the table.

"Thanks."

She sat across from him while he drank his water as instructed.

"City boy?" she said.

"Belgrade."

"What do you do?"

"I'm a musician."

"Not much singing around here."

He put the glass down. She was staring at the rifle that he held across his knees.

"Your lock is off."

He made a reflex move to button up his fly and she doubled over with laughter.

"Boy, did we waste our money."

He laughed too. It was a strange sensation.

"Is this your gun?" he pointed at the pistol.

She nodded. "My father got it. It even has a silencer."

"You know a lot about guns."

"I knew nothing until recently. Would you like some coffee?"

"I haven't had one in days. I don't know if I should."

"Your stomach is probably fine now. It was just fear. Let me ask my folks if they'd like some, too."

There was an icon of Saint George on the wall above the television in the corner, hung so close to the set that it was impossible to watch anything on it without seeing the icon at the same time. On the shelf under the screen was a photo album, and Johnny toyed with the thought of getting up and flipping through it, but he still felt nauseated and decided to sit still. He noticed several German tabloids next to the album. Great—people are fucking, divorcing, and getting high elsewhere. The night is narrow, the night is always local.

She returned with some empty brandy glasses in her hand. "They don't want any," she said, heading to the kitchen. "I'll fix some for the two of us."

He stood up and went after her.

As she found the cups and sugar in an old sideboard, he asked, "Did you say 'money' before?"

She put a small pan on the stove. "Yes."

"What did you mean?"

"Well, you've been hired to keep us safe."

"Hired?"

"Paid."

"I wasn't paid. I was conscripted. They brought us here."

"Bullshit. The truce is holding, but some Croatian paramilitaries wander around killing Serbs. We didn't have much faith in the army so we looked for someone to hire. The Candyman was paid. The majority of people here have someone working abroad and we raised the money easily. We gave the Candyman half in advance. Ask for your share."

Johnny felt the adrenaline surging into his temples. "Look at me. Look at my hands. I play guitar, damn it! Do you think I would be vomiting after seeing a dead man if I was with them? I'm telling you: I was kidnapped, for fuck's sake!"

She took a step back.

"It doesn't matter what you think of me, but don't say I'm one of them."

"I don't care if you're with them or not, just don't yell," she said. "If you're not with them, they shouldn't hear you."

Johnny sat down at the table. "I've got to go home. I've got to."

"Don't we all?"

Some time after one in the morning, the village was quiet again. It happened in stages, the aural remains of the conflict slowly withdrawing before the sounds that lived here. Johnny and three other soldiers were to sleep in Mira's house that night. The back room was small and windowless with a concrete floor. Apparently it was a storage space but it felt safe, and after some straw was laid on top of the concrete, it felt warm.

As his comrades snored, Johnny pondered.

The whole action had been surprisingly short. Shots had been fired from many guns outside the village with only five or six guns responding. After half an hour or so, three of the Croatian paramilitaries had been found dead—as was reported by the Candyman's people—and two had been caught trying to sneak through the woods. The rest, it was said, had run away. Strange, no one made a big fuss about those who had disappeared. According to the numbers that Pap had reported, some thirty combatants had vanished. Could they not warn their forces in the next village, only a few miles away? Could they not, then, attack in a few hours, tonight? Lies. Again. Johnny tried to see the time on his Rolex, but no light shone through the open door and he gave up.

MACHINE. *December 14, 1992*

Morning came wrapped up in fog, ironing the place into an ugly mass of colourless shapes. Johnny stood by the front gate wondering where to go. A giant shadow thickened as it approached. He recognized Black.

"Lost your virginity, eh?"

Johnny's back straightened a little.

"What do you say? Do you like the smell of shooting now?"

Johnny scratched the stubble on his chin. "Do you have any idea where can I find Pap?"

"It's easy, man. Always look for bosses in the safest area—in this case the house in the middle of the village, the big orange one. I just came from there."

Black looked inquisitively at the square grey shape behind Johnny. "You slept here? Comfy?"

"Not really," Johnny said. "They put us into a storage room without windows. Black, I found a dead civilian last night. There weren't any weapons on him, and it looked as if he was shot in the back."

Black slowly put two fingers into his pocket, took out a pack of gum, pulled out a piece and unwrapped it. "I told you not to look around too much, didn't I," he finally said, putting the gum into his mouth.

"This is business, right, this whole thing?"

Black squinted at him. "Who told you that?"

"It doesn't matter. I know."

Black sighed. "This is a machine, Johnny. We can't have a gear turning in the opposite direction to everything else.

Its teeth will get broken right away. If you even hiss about this to anyone else, that's it, you understand?"

Johnny opened his mouth, than changed his mind and just nodded.

"Be serious about it, man. All right?" Black disappeared into the fog.

A few minutes later, Johnny was in front of the largest building in the village. Two Black Lions stood guard by the door.

"I'm here to see Pap," he said. The men waved him inside.

The hall was more silent that Johnny had expected. There were no radio sounds, no telephones ringing, nothing that would make the soundscape of a command post. A woman in a black scarf appeared from the back of the house, carrying a tray with coffee cups and brandy glasses. She went through a door on his left and he went after her. Pap was sitting with one of the sergeants and a stocky man in his early sixties.

"Ah, now we shall have a concert to celebrate the victory," Pap said when he saw Johnny. "Come, sit with us. This is our host, Mr. Marko."

The man nodded without extending his hand.

"I'm sorry, Captain, I don't mean to intrude. Can I have a word with you, please? It's urgent."

"Urgent? I don't hear any shots outside."

"I have information you would want to know, Captain."

"All right."

Pap got up and led him down the corridor to some sort of an office, with a typewriter and fax machine on the desk in the corner.

"Sit," said Pap. "What is it?"

"One of the locals told me last night that the village has paid the Candyman for protection. They gave him half in advance. I don't know who we fought last night but there were fewer of them than you told us to expect. I'm thinking we've all been caught in the Candyman's net."

"They didn't say how much money was involved?"

"No. But I could probably find out, if you wish."

"Leave it to me," Pap said. "We don't know who to trust here. Don't talk to anyone about this. You haven't so far, I hope?"

"No," said Johnny.

"Good. If this is true, my friend, we shall take a trip to Belgrade, the two of us. I have some high-level talking to do."

The rest of the day dragged by. After leaving the orange house, Johnny went for a walk. As the wind lifted the fog in long, slow waves, the village appeared—two rows of serious houses on the sides of the wide road with several short cross streets leading nowhere in particular. Why do people live in such places? He had been through villages with gardens, orchards, wells, beauty, and had always been able to understand their attraction, but this was a mutant. It was as if its inhabitants' rationale was simply to outdo their neighbours, building ever larger, uglier buildings. This was the germinating seed of an ugly town, and—after he stumbled upon that thought in his head—the violence from the previous night suddenly seemed understandable. Not understandable, he corrected himself, but logical. If you decide to build several ugly houses together with the idea that they will grow into an ugly town, why not expect violence? Ugliness oozes aggression.

He passed a bar already full of soldiers and paramilitaries and went into a small place on one of the side streets. Two older men were sitting at a corner table, drinking coffee and shots of brandy, and a serious-looking woman tended bar. He ordered some eggs and bacon, sat in the opposite corner from the men, and took out his notebook. He ate his breakfast slowly, and then drank a coffee, without being able to come up with a single word. Anything he put down on paper would fortify this place in his memory and he did not want that to happen. Finally, he closed the notebook and put it back in his pocket. One of the old men, in a red-checkered shirt that looked like a member of the family of tablecloths, had been glancing at him every so often. Now that the bridge was open, he said, "Where are you from, son?"

"From Belgrade, grandpa. How is life here?"

"Why, are you thinking of moving?"

Johnny saw the mischievous shine in his eye, and smiled. "Everything's possible."

"Not now, it isn't," the man's companion said. A pair of glasses protruded from the breast pocket of his ancient jacket, and his bushy eyebrows connected above his nose.

"Join us," said Tablecloth Shirt.

Johnny took his cup and moved to their table. "How did you sleep last night?"

"Like the princess on the pea," said Tablecloth Shirt. "There must have been a bullet under my mattress."

He and Johnny laughed. Eyebrows remained serious.

"This looks like a rich village," Johnny said.

"People here are hard-working, son. Almost every house has someone in Germany or Austria. They intend to come back when they retire."

"Are there mixed marriages?"

"A few," Eyebrows said. "We used to live nicely with one another before this started. Then the idiots came to power. When fools are riding, everyone turns into an ass."

Tablecloth Shirt moved his legs under the table.

"Don't give me any signals," Eyebrows said. "This is my place and I'm free to speak as I wish."

"Don't worry, I'm not one of them—I'm here by mistake," Johnny said.

"See? He's here by mistake," Eyebrows said. "No," he said to Johnny, "*I'm* here by mistake. I was against this deal. Yeah, there were some fools with guns here, some Croatian boys, but they weren't doing any harm—this is one of the villages where Serbs are in the majority. Then that idiot Marko decided to bring you in so we can sleep well. I sleep well anyway. I've never harmed anyone in my life."

"No incidents before we got here?"

"None," Eyebrows concluded, offering this as definitive proof.

"I was told that the Croatian paramilitaries killed someone two nights ago."

"Not in this village, son," Tablecloth Shirt said. "Perhaps somewhere else."

"What will happen," Eyebrows said, "is that now that you are here, they will start paying attention to our village. You'll see. Weapons draw weapons."

CRACKLE. *December 15, 1992*

Sara sat at her desk next to the window, one hand on the questionnaires from the embassy, her chin resting on the other. It was evening, cold and wet. She did not really want to finish the questionnaires right now, but neither did she feel like going out. Earlier, she had walked to a small store two blocks away, passing through the pedestrian zone of Knez Mihailova Street. The city felt strange. Normally, at this time of year, Belgrade would be filled with lights and laughter, with people hurrying to buy presents. Now, the city seemed undecided as to whether to get ready for the holidays as usual or bow its head in silence. Or perhaps that was her situation. Boris's connections had not come up with any new information, and she still could neither negate nor confirm the rumour that she had overheard that night at the awards.

She peeked under the bandage on her palm. The cuts were almost healed but she kept them covered to remind her to keep her hand out of trouble.

Why Canada? Because you can cut out your own space, Boris had said. When you go to a country in Europe, you feel that if you are lucky you can fit in but not change anything there. In the countries of the New World—Canada, New Zealand, Australia, even the States—nothing has been finalized yet. Not only can you fit in, you can change it. You can make a place that is brand new, yours only. You can leave an imprint.

If she filled in the questionnaire tonight she would be doing something for Johnny. Now that this thing had happened, his being drafted and all, she expected that he, too, would want to apply for exit papers. She had asked Boris for two applications, which he brought back from the Canadian embassy for her. Hers was done except for one question. How did you answer: "Have you taken part, in any way, in the current armed conflict?"

She could lie about it. One flat "No" and that would be that. The Yugoslav Army hardly shared their lists with foreign embassies. But she had heard that the Canadians had their ways of checking these things, and that even a white lie would mean the application wouldn't be processed. How could she write a no when she felt that everyone and everything had been affected by this war, and that there was not a single soul in the country who had not taken part in some way?

That was the problem with such documents—only a single space for an answer that was so difficult. What about those people like Johnny, like herself, who needed more space?

Boris told her that their chances of getting their Canadian papers would be higher if they were married. Why had they not married yet?

Behind Sara, a record spun on the turntable. Some Croatian friends had given it to her a few years earlier—an old album of Amália Rodrigues. Her voice was like a flame and her phrasing was beyond description. How can one describe the way a funeral pyre burns? The crackling of the record, played so many times it was a small miracle that the needle still stuck in the grooves, was somehow appropriate. It was precisely how a good film director would use an old record in a wartime love scene. Sara could almost see a candle in the window, the light that would lead the missing back . . .

"Shit!" she said aloud. "Shit, shit, shit!"

She stood up and carefully lifted the needle, then turned the amplifier off.

DARK HOUSE. *December 22, 1992*

Life in the village assumed some form of order. Aside from guard shifts and occasional briefings, there wasn't much else to do except engage in cruel practical jokes—funny here, too scatological to take home. Three Croatian families decided to move out, and were allowed to go once they agreed to leave everything except their personal belongings behind. The rest of the Croats in the village decided to stay after Pap gave them guarantees that they would be protected. Two nights later, a truck with Serbian plates parked outside one of the deserted homes, and several Lions moved everything saleable from the house into the truck. The same thing happened with the other two homes. Four more unmarked trucks were parked just outside the village, and the Lions stood guard over them—perhaps they were already full of loot and waiting to form a convoy to Serbia.

Once a day, sometimes twice, the level of alert was raised because of suspicious activities on the Croatian side, but nothing ever happened. Johnny assumed that this was the way to keep fighters less drunk. But the frequent alerts took a toll: arguments broke out between soldiers and Lions and, two days earlier, some drunken conscripts had got into a fight with a couple of villagers. As a result, Pap decided to form a unit of military police. Johnny's name was on the list with several others. They were supposed to patrol regularly and were entitled to make arrests on the spot.

The night he became an MP, Johnny dined at Mira's house. Her mother had chased everyone out of the kitchen so she could have it to herself, so Mira invited Johnny to her room on the upper floor. A TV stood on a glass shelf in the corner, and below it a row of videotapes. A small wardrobe was behind the door, and next to it a makeup stand with a large mirror. Mira left the door open and they sat on the bed by the window.

Mira's father was a stocky man in his fifties, his face full of lines. When he had met Johnny for the first time a half-hour earlier, he had not introduced himself—this was his house.

"What do your parents do?" Johnny said.

"They both worked in Germany for twenty-two years," Mira said. "Dad started building this house five years ago, so they could come back after retiring and be somebodies. Then they decided to return while they were still strong, to start a pig farm. They both came just two months before the first gun was fired. Great timing, huh?"

"You stayed in Germany?"

"I have a boyfriend in Munich, and they did not want to jeopardize my future with him."

"Are you getting married?"

She shrugged. "We have a long way to go before we've earned enough to start a life on our own."

"What do you do there?"

"I work in an electronics store."

"Why did you come back?"

"I wanted to persuade them to come back to Germany with me. My father got me a gun instead. They have an arsenal in the basement. Let me show you."

He followed her downstairs.

"So you're a policeman now, huh? That's a shitty job, right?"

"Why?"

"Well, who will you dare to arrest, really, when everyone is armed? I think it's throwing sand in our eyes."

She unlocked the heavy door and switched on the lights. The basement was built like a bunker with concrete walls and narrow windows. It had a bathroom in one corner and three chest freezers along a wall. A heavy walnut cabinet stood on the opposite wall. She opened it. Inside, there was a brand-new Kalashnikov, two rifles, several hand grenades, and five or six pistols, some of them large.

"Some pig farm," Mira said. "But, you know what they say—'Protect yourself and God will protect you.'" She chuckled. "What about your parents?"

"They died in a train crash."

"How old were you?"

"Ten."

"Where did you live afterwards?"

"Don't be offended, but why does it matter?"

Mira nodded. "You've turned out well, considering."

"Considering what?"

"I have a friend with a similar story. He is very soft, insecure. It spoiled him, I guess."

"Could be. I meant to ask you something. I tried calling Belgrade, but I can't get through. Is it only this village?"

"No. The lines are cut between Croatia and Serbia. Why? You want to call your girlfriend?"

Mira's mother called down the stairs to tell them dinner was ready.

The snow started drifting down around ten the next morning. The size of the flakes kept increasing, until, by noon, it finally looked like what it was, a winter storm.

Johnny's three-man patrol started their shift at eight in the evening. By then, the wind had stopped, the snow had finished, the stars appeared, and the village looked ready for the coming holidays and unprepared for war. The soldiers, except for those standing guard on the outskirts of the village, were mostly inside—in the bar, in the houses where they slept watching the news or playing cards.

"Why the fuck are we doing this?" Goran asked. He was a tall, muscular man in his early thirties, a judo instructor from a small town south of Belgrade. "The men will have a few drinks and if they get into a fight, they're all smart enough to leave the weapons out of it. The locals are all at home."

"How about *we* get something to drink? We'll be freezing our asses off out there." Mile was the company joker, the oldest of the conscripts. He was a farmer in his early forties, stocky, with a crooked nose. Pap had apparently selected his policemen according to their size and strength.

"No way, man," Johnny said. "Someone has to keep his head clear. People are really bored now and that's dangerous."

"All right, boss," said Mile. "You city folks don't know how to enjoy life. If I were commanding this patrol, we would be sitting next to a furnace, I can tell you that. With women in our laps and drinks in our hands."

Johnny did not respond. This was indeed a shitty job, but at least it was useful. Many of his fellow soldiers were not at all happy about those Croatian houses being ransacked by the Lions. He had no doubt that if the tension got too bad they would bring weapons into it, and he knew who would be the first to use them.

The temperature was dropping, and the sound of their steps on the snow-covered streets was changing from croaks to cracks. Wood smoke rose straight from the chimneys. The other patrol was supposed to visit all five local joints, and Johnny and his men were to make sure that the streets were safe. Five watering holes in such a small place.

They came to an intersection and—since the main street was lit well enough to see that it was empty—Johnny turned right onto the side street and his companions followed. In the window of a butcher store on the corner was a handwritten note regarding services at the Catholic church in the next village, which meant the owners were Croats.

Muffled voices came from television sets behind the closed windows and drawn curtains. This street also looked deserted. When they had walked down half of it, Johnny stopped.

"The only place this leads is to the fields. Let's go back."

"Sure, boss," Mile said loudly. Looking over Johnny's shoulder, he added, quietly, "There's someone at the end of the street."

Johnny turned and squinted. He saw it now: an illogical shadow at the end of the left row of houses. Among parallel lines—windows, facades, fences, doors—it was rounded enough to be a person. A person trying to remain invisible.

"Against the wall," hissed Johnny, and in a few steps all three of them were pressed against the closest house on the same side of the street as the shadow. "Arms ready," Johnny said, pulling out his semi-automatic pistol and sneaking ahead.

One of the wooden fences between them and the shadow was broken in the middle. It leaned towards the street, making the silhouette invisible. Poking his head around, Johnny was startled when a small flame burst from the direction of their target, maybe twenty yards away. For a moment, Johnny expected to hear a shot, and then he realized the man was lighting a cigarette.

"Don't move," Johnny called, surprising himself by the flatness of his voice. "Who are you?"

For a few seconds there was no answer. The man held the match flame close to his face long enough for Johnny to recognize the Lion they called the Boxer. Except for his broken nose, skinny little Boxer didn't fit the description. He was probably a small-time crook here for what he could pillage. The matchstick burned his fingers. He cursed in a muffled voice, dropping it.

"Why the fuck are you sneaking up?" he said to Johnny as he blew on his fingers.

"What are you doing here?" Johnny asked, his two comrades at his side. The Boxer noticed the guns.

"Hey, put the guns away—are you insane? We're on the same side, idiots."

The two other men holstered their weapons but Johnny just lowered his pistol.

"So, why are you here, Boxer?"

"What do you care?" He noticed the white belts on their uniforms. "Oh, right. The cops. I'm scared shitless."

"Are you standing guard?"

"You're crazy."

Johnny craned to look behind him through a narrow side gate to the last house in the row. It was dark. No other house in the village was dark this early.

"Step aside," Johnny said.

"What, you're going to rob the Croats now? Better do it in daylight so you can see what they're hiding."

"How do you know they're Croats?" Johnny raised his gun again. "Step aside!"

The man obliged.

"Mile, stay here and make sure he doesn't make a sound."

"No problem, boss."

"What, this peasant will stop me?" The Boxer frowned.

Mile raised his left fist from the hip and decked the Lion, who almost lost his footing. "If you want, I can nail you to the gate so you won't slip again," Mile said.

"Goran, come with me." Johnny pushed the gate open, the wood scraping on the ice below. At the corner of the house, he waved Goran ahead to check one side. The man sneaked to the window on the ground floor and carefully looked inside. Then he crept along to a small basement window out of which a faint light shone, and knelt to look in. After a moment, he gestured to Johnny to come.

Over Goran's shoulder, Johnny saw a young woman on the edge of a bed, naked. A man was holding her legs on his shoulders, raping her. His moves were merciless. Two men sat next to them, watching. One of them, with a black bandana, held a gun in the girl's mouth. The other one had unbuttoned his black uniform pants, waiting his turn. There was no sound, just the faces: the insanity on the face of the rapist, the grinning of the two other men, the numb stare on the girl's face.

Johnny touched Goran's shoulder. They got up and moved quickly towards the corner of the house. Clear. They came to the side entrance and Goran carefully pressed the latch. It was open. He stood for a few seconds, listening, and then entered. Johnny went in after him and saw the stairs leading to the basement. He motioned for Goran to check the rest of the house, and he went downstairs.

At the bottom was a short corridor with two doors, both closed. He leaned his ear against one of them and heard the slapping of skin against skin. Slowly, he pressed the handle and pushed a little. The hinges were silent. He raised his gun to eye level, and hit the door with his boot. It banged against something and he yelled, "Don't move!"

Nothing much happened. The gun was still inside the girl's mouth and Johnny did not really know what to do next.

"Hey, look," said the Lion holding the gun. "It's the soldier with the ponytail. Hey, bro, is that tail too high or are you really shitting from your brain?"

The other two laughed.

"Some people really have no manners. Who taught you to interrupt people when they are having sex?" the rapist said.

Johnny did not like the grin on his face.

"Leave the girl," Johnny said, aiming straight at his head. "You are all under arrest."

"I think he's serious," said the first Lion, not moving the gun.

"Yup. See the sweat?" the unbuttoned Lion said.

Johnny felt the drops gathering on his forehead. "I'll shoot if I have to," he said.

"Hey, shithead, what better death than to die fucking? Watch me and jerk, moron." The rapist made a forceful thrust with his hips. The girl moaned. "You see? She's enjoying it. Croatian pussies like it rough." He continued to move inside her. "Tell him, bro, while I fill her up, tell him what we discovered."

"This little whore has a brother but he's not at home," the unbuttoned Lion said. "Their parents couldn't tell us where he was, so we came down here to ask her. We think he's with the Croatian throat cutters. So we decided to make her a small Serb, to spread the love. You should stick it in, too, if you're a man. She won't tell anyone."

A door slammed on the upper floor and feet padded down the stairs. Goran appeared behind Johnny.

"Her parents are upstairs. Beaten unconscious and tied up," he said to Johnny. "You pricks have a problem. Get that gun out of her mouth and step aside."

The rapist grinned at him. "The gun is staying. As is my dick."

Goran crossed the room in two steps and hit the rapist

so hard that he was out before he landed on the one holding the gun, knocking him to the floor. The unbuttoned
Lion went for Goran, who did something with his hands,
spun him around, and threw him on the floor. A gun went
off. The Lion with the bandana had pulled himself out
from under his friend and was now trying for a better
angle on Goran. Johnny fired. The man dropped his gun
and clutched at his biceps. Blood flowed through his fingers and he moaned.

"Did he get you?" Johnny asked.

Goran shook his head as he helped the girl sit up.

Johnny pulled the blanket from the foot of the bed and
wrapped it around the girl's shoulders. She was shivering
now, but still silent.

"Take her upstairs. Tell Mile to bring the Boxer here. We'll
tie them all up. Find a phone and call Pap to send more men."

Goran gave the girl his shoulder to lean on. Johnny
flicked on the light and picked up the weapons. He found a
table lamp with a long cord, yanked it out, and began tying
up the Lions.

It was several hours before the whole mess was over. The
wounded Lion was only scratched, it turned out. Just before
Johnny left headquarters, the Candyman turned up from
somewhere, furious, and locked himself up with Pap. The
prisoners were soon taken out, handcuffed, and put in one
of the Candyman's trucks. Then the truck and two Jeeps
roared off into the night. By that point the whole village
had heard the news and there wasn't a single house whose
windows were completely dark at one in the morning.

The storeroom at Mira's house was empty when Johnny got back. He was grateful that the other conscripts were on guard duty—he didn't feel like talking to anyone. He lay down in the dark, in his uniform, and tried not to think.

When he woke up it was still dark and he could hear snoring around him. He got up and stepped over the sleeping soldiers, trying not to wake them. The house was silent. At the back door, he put his boots back on and went outside. The village was lit only by the moon and the houses around him looked like containers waiting for their ship. He leaned against the wall. It took him a few moments to notice a small orange dot to his right. The dot went higher and intensified. He recognized the lips and the nose.

"Want some?" Mira whispered.

He smelled the pot in the air and extended his hand. Their fingers touched as she passed the joint. He inhaled a couple of times, covering the glow with his hand, and offered it back to her.

"Finish it," she said. "I'm fine."

His eyes had became accustomed to the darkness and he glanced sideways at her. She was sitting on a bench along the wall, her legs outstretched, her face lifted towards the starry sky. He sat next to her. The pot started working. It was not a downer, apparently, but it did not lift him up either. He felt heavier and his shoulders fell a little. He took the last drag, burning his fingers, and then extinguished the roach in the snow.

"That girl, tonight. She's a friend of mine," she said.

Her head moved towards his shoulder so slowly that he was not sure if she had fallen asleep or just wanted to lean on him. Then he felt her tongue on his neck. He let her slide it towards his ear and when she bit him gently, he turned to her, took her face with his hand, and opened her lips with his tongue. It was a slow, deep kiss. He felt oddly surprised by the slowness, as if the war had dictated urgency and despair and they were doing this the wrong way. He felt her hand on his crotch and helped her unbutton his pants. It was easy for her fingers to find their way through his military underwear, with no buttons and a long slit in front. He briefly felt cold on his dick as she pulled it out. Then a warm palm protected him, and she lowered her head and took him into her mouth. As he leaned his head against the wall, his last distinguishable thought was that he was alive.

LIKE LOVE. *December 23, 1992*

"I think it's better if I relieve the three of you from patrol right now," Pap said. "The Candyman isn't happy and neither are his people. Frankly, I think he feels humiliated. I wouldn't want to be in the skin of those monkeys that you arrested. Not because of what they did, but because they allowed themselves to be arrested by reservists."

Johnny remained silent. Pap and he were alone in the office of the orange house.

"Until the dust settles, you can stand guard on the outskirts of the village and sleep in the outpost with a few other soldiers just in case. You do understand it's for your safety?"

Johnny nodded.

Pap sighed. "I would recommend you for some sort of honour but you don't want people to know you're here. That's fine—we don't want them to know we're here either. Later we can reward you for something done on Serbian territory. The catch is that it must be made public and then you become a symbol for the media. Is that okay with you? You're an idol to the kids anyway, why not add to it?"

Johnny lowered his head. "There's nothing I need to be rewarded for," he said. "They were torturing that girl. They would probably have killed her in the end. And Goran deserves the reward more than I do."

Pap nodded. "Very good answer. Okay then, Goran it will be. You're free to go."

Johnny turned to leave, then said, "Captain?"

"Yes?"

"It's not the uniform. It's not war. It's this particular war. I can't tell my fans that any of this is okay."

Pap did not answer.

The streets were deserted. It was quarter to eleven. What do people do in a place like this? No public library, no bowling alley, no shopping area, only local joints. Some of them had television sets but they played the news all the time, and all the news was as ugly as usual, more than usual.

Johnny decided to go back to the small place where he had met Eyebrows and Tablecloth Shirt. There was nobody in the restaurant when he entered. The serious woman brought his coffee, a piece of bread, and several boiled eggs on a platter. She put them on the table and went back behind the bar without a word. He saw some old magazines on the shelf under the TV, got up and picked a few to flip through. Bill Clinton, New American President. The gun in the hairy hand, the absolute horror of helplessness on the girl's face. Her lips around the steel. The Federal Assembly of Czechoslovakia had voted to split the country in two: Couldn't we have an amicable divorce, too? He raised his head, stared through the window at the deserted, ice-covered street. The girl will be fine. Time heals everything. No—time is only a reef that slows down the waves of memories. The girl will be fine. She has to be fine. The only thing that pleased him was the aggression afterwards— Goran's moves, the blood, the tight, tight cord around the men's hands. Kicking them before the backup arrived. Yes, kicking them in the sides, in the knees, pistol-whipping the one who shot at Goran. He did that. And Mile let him go on longer than needed, dangerously long, before pulling him away and calming him down.

Mira had been in the back of his mind since he woke up. He was not sure of the way she was present in him. He knew how she wasn't. Not as love—but not as a notch, either. He had never hidden anything from Sara. She knew how rock tours operate, and told him that she did not want to hear any details from him. And, she said, if she ever heard details *about* him, that would mean the end. But Johnny loved her and there had been nothing to hide until now. Until now? Had he already decided to hide it? He was surprised by how some autonomous male centre in his brain had retreated into defensive mode. Mira had not chosen him last night. The night had chosen him. The ugliness, the horror. And for those same reasons, he let it happen.

Half an hour later, he was in Mira's house. She was out, so he went to the storage room, took his shaving kit from his backpack, and headed for the bathroom. Another soldier came out as he was approaching.

"Johnny," he said. "We're standing guard tonight. I have it written down somewhere who goes where, but I think you're in the woods. Get some sleep."

Johnny took a long shower. When he finished he found Mira in the living room. She was reading one of the German magazines, a coffee cup in front of her.

She asked, "Are you hungry?" Her face showed no emotion, but her question made him blink. It was so simple, so basic, yet nobody had asked him for such a long time.

"I've already eaten," he said.

"You didn't have to—we're supposed to feed you."

He sat next to her. "Are you okay?"

"You mean about last night? Are you?" Her look pierced him.

"I have a girlfriend back in Belgrade. I never—"

"Neither have I," she said. "I have a boyfriend in Munich. So if you ever have a gig there, be careful what you say between songs."

Their eyes locked, longer than he had planned. Hers were serious, and blue, and just a tad shinier than normal. He hugged her.

"Thanks," he whispered.

She smiled at him. "Maybe we didn't waste our money after all."

"Seriously," Johnny said, letting go. "Thanks."

Before she could say anything more, her father entered. "I hear you're on guard tonight," he said. "We'll keep it quiet around here so you can get some sleep."

Around seven, Mira's father woke the four of them up. They had dinner with the family, and then they picked up their guns and went to the orange house, where a sergeant gave them instructions. It was a little after eight when they took over for their four-hour shift.

Johnny did not like his position but there was nothing he could do about it. The forest started some three hundred yards from the last house to the south, unfolding by the side of the local road. It wasn't large, probably a few hundred yards in diameter, but there were also small patches of trees farther south and west. If someone wanted to enter the village unnoticed, this was the best way.

The wind created enough of a murmur in the trees to keep him on his toes, but there were also small animal sounds, birds, voices drifting from the village, music and laughter. . . . How would he be able to detect steps approaching in the night? After half an hour, he was able to distinguish the sounds better, but every now and then he heard a strange noise that more often than not sounded like a cautious footfall.

He was supposed to remain standing so he wouldn't fall asleep but also so that the officer who brought the change of guard would see him from a safe distance. Still, after thinking he heard slow steps for the third time, he improvised a seat from fallen branches and lowered himself behind one of the bigger trees. Looking up, he could see the stars through the branches. He tried not to think of the time.

Time was against them, thought Sara. No matter how hard they fought not to think about it, even the name of the restaurant reminded them: the Last Chance. It was in the park next to the state television building, and although they could have met at other places in the vicinity, they decided on the Last Chance simply because that was the place they used to go when they all still worked for Belgrade Television.

Although more journalists and editors were being suspended every month, fewer people were showing up for these sessions at the bar. Sara realized why after half an hour of sitting in the shabby room full of smoke, surrounded by former colleagues who were drinking much more than they had the month before. They were all acting as if it was due to the coming holidays, but she knew better. When you are a journalist, you are a junkie. Your whole system depends on the daily input of news and—equally important, if not more—your output of digested information. Having only the input with no means of giving it back had started to eat all of them from the inside out.

The noise was unbearable. People kept interrupting one another, cracking jokes that nobody found funny. Yet everyone laughed loudly. Sara ordered a cognac simply because she wanted to do what everyone else did. Her corner of December had been agonizingly quiet and she had hoped that by coming here she would find a little harmless distraction. Besides, these people were still among the best informed in Belgrade and might have heard something about Johnny.

Miki was a freelancer who came to the regular bar nights to show support, he said. He specialized in war zones. For several years now, he had had no problem selling his footage to whomever he chose. He had covered the Gulf, the Tuareg rebellion, the civil wars in Algeria, Georgia, and Sierra Leone, and he had just returned from Tajikistan. The only conflict he refused to cover was this one in Yugoslavia. When a producer from CNN asked him why, he responded that he would not be able to go to the front without taking a gun and shooting at everyone involved. "I can't stand people with guns in the orchards" was the sentence that was often quoted in the Western media and brought him some sort of fame.

He and two other women—Vesna and Gordana—were sitting at Sara's table. The women were showing signs of considerable interest in Miki, their backs straight, their voices a touch more husky than usual. Either he was accustomed to this, or else he did not want to show that he noticed, or perhaps he was not interested—Sara could not decide which. As usual in Belgrade, after the Western media turned their attention to his work, Miki's popularity surged. He was praised not only for his courage and his integrity but for his rugged good looks, his long black hair, his build, his hands that could strangle a bear yet were so gentle to the touch. Nobody was exactly sure who he did touch, however, since he guarded his privacy and was rarely seen at parties.

But tonight he was here and talking mostly to Sara. At first she did not notice, but the other women started giving her looks. When Miki excused himself and went towards the bathroom at the back of the restaurant, Vesna said, with a hint of envy in her voice, "Sara, he's ripe."

"He reminds me of Johnny," Gordana added.

"Don't be mean, darling, "Vesna said. "He's totally different."

"Well, not so much physically. But he's also an alpha male and, you know, he's a fighter, too."

"Darling, you wouldn't put up a fight."

They all laughed. It was true, Miki did have something in common with Johnny—Sara felt that, too. Miki's reports were brutally honest, just like Johnny's music, and had some poetry to them too.

A waiter brought another round of drinks to their table as Miki returned, and the next half-hour passed in friendly banter. When the two women excused themselves to go and sit with another group, Sara suddenly felt exposed. Miki's eyes kept falling somewhere in the area of her lips and she could not help but notice sporadic glances from the others. He must have noticed too since he said, "Why don't we take a walk?"

She thought about it for a moment. Everybody would see them leaving and everyone would think the same thing. But really, who cared? Miki paid the bill, and they left the Last Chance.

In the small park, only a few dog walkers braved the cold.

"Sara, why don't you come and work with me?" Miki said.

"Work for you?" she repeated.

"Not for me, *with* me. There is plenty of stuff you could do, everything from research to going on camera. You know how I hate talking to the lens."

When she was silent, he added, "You do know they won't take you back, not while this war is going on, right?"

"I know. But if I start working for someone else, they will take that as an excuse to cut me off completely. If I get foreign money, that will be that. And what about when this is all over? Then what?"

"You could work as a fixer for some of the correspondents. They would pay very well to have someone like you. Nobody will know."

"Miki. It's so easy to soil your diapers. I will know. I need to live with what I do."

They left the park to cross the Boulevard of Revolution.

"Is it Johnny?" he said.

"What about Johnny?"

"You know. The stories."

"About him being with the Candyman? I've heard them, yes. Do you really believe he would do it?" She had intended this ironically but it didn't come out that way.

"In a war God dies with the first shot. You cannot trust people, and there is no truth in anything. The animal in us eventually leads us to survival, nothing else."

She looked at him sideways. "Aren't you lonely thinking like that?"

"I'm still alive thinking like that."

They walked downhill towards the Yugoslav Drama Theatre. A boy was selling roasted chestnuts on the corner. Sara bought two packets and handed one to Miki.

"Johnny was drafted," she said. "All I know is that he was transferred to some place in the northwest and that's where I lost track of him. Someone is spreading rumours for propaganda reasons. People are refusing to take part in this war so the regime is using its favourite criminals. If they could make young guys believe that the Candyman can recruit people like Johnny, tons of hotheads will volunteer."

"Sara—is he still alive?"

"I would know if he wasn't."

Miki nodded.

"Johnny thinks that war is a time when only faith can save you," Sara said. "Perhaps not in others, perhaps not in God, but you have to believe in your own system. Everyone is screaming at you: warmongers, peaceniks, the media, authorities, terrified people, your children, your parents, everyone. These are deafening times—your own thoughts get stifled in all the noise. I guess that's how your animal starts to lead. The only way to silence all those screams is to listen to yourself carefully. Deep down, each one of us knows who we are. Stick to that, and you'll be fine. That is part of the reason why I believe Johnny is fine—I know that he always hears his inner voice."

"I hope, for his own good, that Johnny is more cynical than that."

She laughed.

Miki took a pair of gloves from one of the many pockets in his jacket. "It's freezing out here," he said. "How about another drink?"

Johnny could not stand the cold anymore. No matter how

many branches he piled beneath himself, he still felt the snow. He was sorry that he had not taken the advice of one of his comrades and brought a hip flask with him. But no matter how ridiculous this all seemed, it was still a war, and he wanted to keep his head clear.

By the degree of numbness in his feet, he decided he must have been out here for three hours at least. He started doing squats and then froze, reacting to something he could not yet quite sense. He raised his gun to his chest, released the safety as inaudibly as he could, and held his breath. The normal murmur of the forest had returned. Still, he lay down slowly behind a fallen trunk. There was that sound again: this time he was sure of it—a large animal, or a man. Slow steps, very careful, a few seconds between each one. Then a bunch of stars disappeared behind a human silhouette. The officer in charge would not approach like this. Johnny took aim. He inhaled deeply, and just before he yelled a warning into the night, the silhouette quietly called his name.

Again: "Johnny?"

"Who is it?" he whispered back.

"It's me, Black. Where are you?"

Still pointing his gun, Johnny stood up. "Over here."

"You fucking scared me, bro. You're not where you're supposed to be. I thought maybe someone got you."

"What are you doing here?"

"This is the only place where we can talk in private. And it's freezing, so I brought you a little something to keep you warm."

He sat down on the tree trunk, pulled out a bottle from the inside of his coat, took a swig and handed it over.

Johnny wiped the bottle's mouth against his sleeve, and drank. The sharp punch of the homemade brandy warmed him up. He handed the bottle back.

"The Candyman's first reaction was to eliminate you, bro."

Black was clearly waiting for a reaction, so Johnny said, "Eliminate me?"

"Yeah. But I told him he was overreacting. You're not an idiot, I told him. You had to do what you did. There were two people with you—you couldn't have pretended our guys were not doing that pussy. I told him that for our cause you were better alive than dead. I think that's what made him change his mind. I mean, totally change his mind, full circle. To the point that you will get your piece from our little business with the locals. You haven't talked to anyone about it, have you? Not Pap, I hope?"

"No."

"That's what I told him. The Candyman. He never trusts anyone. Got a light?"

"You can't smoke here."

"I won't smoke. I've got a paper for you to sign."

Johnny heard rustling inside Black's coat and then there was a sheet of paper in his hand.

"What's that?"

"An oath. I mean, they call it an oath but I think of it as a confidentiality agreement, really. I have a flashlight somewhere, wait, here's a pen, and, oh, okay, here's the light."

Johnny sat next to Black on the trunk and flattened the paper on his knee. Black switched his tiny lamp on, protected it with his other hand, and held it so Johnny could see. As Johnny waited for his eyes to get accustomed to what seemed like a blinding light, someone in the forest yelled, "Stop!" Instinctively, Johnny hit the hand holding the lamp and it shone on Black's chest. A short and sharp sound, like a branch snapping underfoot, came from somewhere near and Black jerked and fell behind the trunk. Johnny reached towards him, lost his balance, and fell too. Another branch cracked, and Johnny clearly heard the whistle of a bullet above his head. A third snap, and a short scream. Johnny was on his back, clutching his gun, his heart thumping in his chest. He looked around. There was no safer place than where he was. Black was making a strange, quiet, gurgling sound.

"Johnny?" someone hissed. He did not recognize the voice.

"Johnny, are you okay?"

"Yes. Who are you?"

"The Commander. Watch the one next to you. Take his weapons away. They came to kill you."

The Commander was what the Black Lions called the Candyman. What was he doing here? And why did he shoot his own soldier? What was that other scream in the forest? Johnny started searching Black and found a handgun in the outside pocket of his coat. He took it and pulled Black's rifle towards him. Then he searched for the tiny lamp. It was next to Black's hand. He switched it on, left it on the tree trunk, and rolled away from it, and farther from Black, who was still making that strange noise.

"Come slowly to where the light hits you," he said. "Don't make any sudden moves or I'll shoot."

A man appeared in the beam. He raised one hand to protect his eyes but there was no doubt about his identity.

"Are you armed?"

"Of course I am," said the Candyman. "If I wasn't you'd be dead by now."

Johnny could not think of any logical retort he could make at this point so he slowly got up, his gun still ready.

"What is this?" he said.

"You chose the wrong person to confide in," the Candyman said. "Pap wasn't happy about you being so well informed." He sat down on the trunk and lit a cigarette. Then he switched off the lamp.

"Who was that in the woods with you?"

"Another of my men. A triple murderer who had recently escaped from jail. I did not trust him, anyway. Too easy to blackmail. That's why your captain chose him."

"Pap sent that man to kill me?"

"Yeah. And Black too. Pap probably offered him a nice sum. Black was a greedy bastard."

"I think he's still alive."

The Candyman listened awhile, then said, "Not for long. His lungs are perforated. Not a nice way to die."

"But why did you—?"

"Save you? I did not come to save you, Johnny, but to punish my men for making deals behind my back. This is my army and I run it like one. I ordered the other one to stop when I found him"—he pointed with his thumb behind his back—"and he made the mistake of turning his gun on me."

Johnny sat down next to him. "Why did it bother Pap

that I knew about the deal? Others probably know about it, too. They live with the locals."

"The locals won't tell—none of them except your little hostess, who is already in a basement. The others know that the deal is off if they tell conscripts about it. Not only would it be off—they would have me as an enemy. They'll keep their mouths shut. Maybe she didn't know the score because she just got here."

"What will you do with her?"

"I intend to keep her locked up as long as we're here, that's what. If you're worried about her pussy, don't be—fucking our clients would be bad for business."

"Those trucks outside the village—protection is not the only business going on here, is it?"

The Candyman puffed on the smoke, then smiled. "I reckon there's no reason not to tell you. They're loaded with weapons and equipment. I'm selling them to Croats."

"To Croats? But—"

"Ah, but of course—you think you know right from wrong, that everything is clear in this war. Well, listen to this: we fought in Croatia last year and we seized those trucks in a village close to the Hungarian border. In them we found all brand-new stuff, and all American. How did the Croats get it when the arms embargo was in place against both sides? That is a question worth five million Deutsche Marks, my friend. The Americans apparently broke the embargo in order to supply their friends. It would be very unpleasant if I took those trucks to Belgrade and opened them in front of the foreign cameras. I don't know who's paying me not to—Yanks or Croats—but I don't care."

"So what about me?"

"I'm still thinking."

Johnny knew the reputation of this man—there was nothing he could do but wait for his fate to be decided. The Candyman had a baby face, gentle eyes, and a kind smile, but some of the stories that circulated in Belgrade claimed that he had already had some ten murders behind him when he started working for the secret police, long before this war. Then he had murdered for them all over Europe, dozens of people—the count was lost in the secret vaults.

"The best solution would be for you to join me. I could keep an eye on you and you would have the best time of your life, I promise you." He laughed. "This is like love: two people who would be a perfect fit but they will never get together. Or I could finish you off right now. All witnesses dead, no one would ever know what happened here. Perhaps my men popped you for arresting their friends. Or the Croats came. Whatever. That's actually very good. Hmm."

Johnny clutched his rifle tighter.

"But I believe in fate. I never wanted to kill you and you survived the attempt on you tonight. But if I let you go, you can't go back to Belgrade. Some people will think you killed our boys and you wouldn't last long. *Your* friends won't like that you've been with my army. If I were you, Johnny, I'd take a hike and start anew."

Johnny sighed. "If this gets reported, they'll catch me when I try crossing the border."

"I'll give you twenty-four hours. And I have a few foreign

passports here. We can take your photo from the military card and you'll be good to go." The Candyman blew out another lungful of smoke. "You have it with you? The military card?"

Johnny found it in his wallet and handed it over.

"You wait here," he said. "I'll send that little slut to bring the passport to you. Make sure she goes back to Germany."

He stood up.

"Should I thank you?" Johnny asked.

"Not at all, not at all. Because this is not over. If you decide to rat against me, remember that I travel fast and can turn up anywhere." Suddenly the Candyman had his handgun pointing at Johnny's forehead. "And then, pop!"

Johnny glimpsed a smile on the man's oddly gentle face, as if the gun belonged to another person, someone who happened to share the same hands. He took Johnny's rifle away from him, put his own gun back into his pocket, and walked towards the man he had killed. He turned Johnny's rifle on the corpse and fired two bullets into it. He then walked to Black's body and shot again.

"Just so I know you won't come back, artist," he said and threw the rifle aside. "It's official now—you've murdered two people."

The Candyman turned to go, but then stopped. "How did you put it in that song of yours? 'I'm fucking my destiny'? Well, the bitch is cheating on you."

He vanished in the night.

NIGHT TRAIN. *December 24, 1992*

It was dawn when Johnny and Mira crossed the Danube into Serbia. She had taken him to her friend's house in another village to find him some civilian clothes and then they were driven to the river, where a man took them across in his motorboat. Two hours later, they boarded a bus from Sombor to Belgrade. At half past ten, they were in Johnny's apartment.

The air was not stale. There were even a few sausages and sardine cans in the fridge. Sara had kept it alive for him.

"You get some rest," he said to Mira. "I need to make some calls. But we should leave today."

"I'll take a shower first, if you don't mind. Where will you go?"

"I haven't decided yet," Johnny said. "What about you?"

"I have enough cash with me to get to Budapest. I'll take a train from there to Munich. You can come with me if you wish. You can stay for a few days in my apartment until you find something."

She did not say, "stay with me."

"Thanks," he said. "But I think I might go to Amsterdam." He had no friends in Amsterdam. But he had been there a few times and it looked Babylonian enough for a fugitive to get lost in it.

He gave her a towel and she closed the bathroom door behind her. He waited until he heard the sound of water and then went to the phone.

Sara felt as if her insides were a broken fridge full of eggs and meat. When she woke up, she dragged herself to the kitchen to make coffee, took a quick shower (was she not supposed to take a long, scalding shower now?), and then put on her bathrobe. She looked briefly in the mirror and pulled the bathrobe up to her chin. She sat at her desk. Her head was throbbing and she downed a painkiller with her coffee. There was nothing in the mail except bills. She switched the radio on and returned to her desk.

She picked up the handset to call someone, then put it back. Her head wanted to separate from her body, because it knew who Miki's hands had touched, and wanted none of it.

The phone rang. At first she thought that it was the tail ring, because she had lifted the handset, but then it rang again. Her mother? Not now. Another ring. Boris? Not now. Miki, for a thank-you chat? Another ring. Someone from her old job? They wanted her back. Not now, not ever. Another. News about Johnny? Bad news? She started crying. Another ring. She picked up and held the handset to her ear, but didn't say anything. The person on the other end was already disconnecting.

Boris stood in front of his bookshelves. This was freakishly difficult. He could take two bags of sixty pounds each with him to Canada, but when he started calculating what he wanted to bring, it added up to something over two hundred pounds. He had to decide fast if he wanted to have enough time to sell some of the stuff he would not be taking with him.

Bulgakov was a no-brainer. He had read *The Master and*

Margarita a dozen times. Varlam Shalamov's *The Kolyma Tales* also had to come. A few comic books, mostly from Pratt's *Corto Maltese* and Magnus and Bunker's *Alan Ford* series. Some of the early *Asterix*. He who loses touch with his childhood is doomed. He'd already filled a good part of one of the suitcases. His eyes skipped to the shelf with the reference books. The Oxford Dictionary? Too big, although it was as important as his passport in the West. He would sell his copy and buy a new one there.

The telephone rang. When he picked it up, Johnny had to say his name twice before he realized who it was. Half an hour later, he was climbing out of a cab in front of Johnny's building.

Johnny cracked the door to check that it was Boris, then let him in. They hugged without words. When they entered the kitchen, Mira was having coffee at the table, her hair still wrapped in a towel.

Boris stood there, waiting for Johnny to say something, but she was faster.

"I'm Mira," she said, extending her hand, "Johnny's 'sister in arms.' " She smiled, putting quotes around her words, and Boris shook her hand and introduced himself. Johnny poured another coffee and put the cup in front of Boris. Then he sat down.

"I don't have much time," he said. "They took us all to Croatia. We were thrown into combat with the Candyman and his men. I can't tell you what happened but the Candyman saved our lives. Mira's and mine. And now I have to run because two of the Candyman's men were killed and he will blame me."

"Jesus, Johnny, slow down a little," said Mira. "Even I don't understand it, and I was there."

Johnny looked at her, then touched Boris's hand. "I'm sorry, man. I'm all fucked up."

Then Johnny retold the story. Boris interrupted occasionally, and Mira filled in the gaps. When he was done, Boris just sat there, smoking and staring into his coffee cup.

After a minute or two, he looked up at Mira, then at his friend. "Did you call Sara?"

"I'll go fix my hair," Mira said and went into the bathroom.

"The first thing this morning. She didn't answer."

"Do you want to try again?"

"No. It was foolish of me to call in the first place. The Candyman promised to give me some time before reporting the murders, but I can't trust him. They could be tapping my phone already."

"Where will you go?" Boris said.

"Amsterdam, probably. Maybe it won't be Amsterdam. But you'll know as soon as I settle down a bit. When the news spreads, there will be two groups after me: some of the Candyman's criminals and the army. The army will almost certainly tap Sara's phone. You have to warn her. We will have to communicate through you until we know more. Is that okay?"

"Don't ask stupid questions."

The hair dryer hummed.

"Johnny, I got Sara two applications for Canadian visas. I think she's filled one in for you."

"I can't make it for the interview, Boris. But that's good.

You two go and I'll find a way to join you. I don't exist anymore, man. I am Robert Dylan now. I can go anywhere but here."

"Robert Dylan?"

"Yeah. That bastard the Candyman has sense of humour, doesn't he?"

"What about her?" Boris pointed his chin in the direction of the bathroom.

"She's going back to Munich. She lives there with her boyfriend."

The hair dryer stopped.

"I can't carry much with me," Johnny said. "You will have to help Sara move my stuff out, and then she should cancel the lease. I'm sorry, man."

"Stop apologizing, Johnny. You're just taking the shortcut. We'll all leave this snakepit."

"We'll get through. We will. Screw the bastards."

"I'll help you pack," said Boris.

"No. I'll do it. You should go. I really am dangerous company now."

They stood for a second, face to face. "Have a happy New Year," Johnny said. They hugged each other and kissed three times.

Train number 340 to Budapest crossed into Hungary at quarter past one that night, after a short, uneventful stop at the border. The two passengers in the second-class compartment of the last carriage sat across from each other by the window, looking out into the dark, unknown land.

RUST

CHAIN OF HAPPY LINKS. *October 16, 1993*

For the couple sitting at the patio table at JoJo's in Yorkville, fourteen degrees Celsius apparently meant chilly. He was dressed in a green raincoat with a thick black lining, boots, and a leather hat. She was in a long brown sheepskin coat, with a woollen shawl around her shoulders and a beret on her head. The passersby were mostly in shirts and jackets, sneakers, although a few young men in T-shirts were probably pushing it. The Canadians did not give up on their summers easily, and a few of those who passed the couple gave them strange looks, as if their clothes would invite winter before its time.

Boris didn't care. Being where nobody knew you was his first taste of perfect freedom.

Until an hour ago, Sara and he had been painting their newly rented apartment. Then they opened all the windows to help the paint dry and came here. Perhaps the draft, when it charged into their living room on the tenth floor, made it seem colder outside than it was. Maybe they overdressed because they had been told that Canada was a cold country, and you want to dance to the right tune. Or it could have been the chill inside of them, from the trip, from the change. This was not a tourist visit, this was the real thing. Emigration—what a thunderous word.

Sara's profile was softened by the shawl, and the beret made her look almost mischievous, but her face was serious. Did she regret? Boris sighed and pulled a cigarette out of the pack. He lit it, inhaled deeply, and let the smoke come slowly out of his mouth.

Rather than thinking of the big leap, Boris had restrained himself to taking a series of small steps—that had been his strategy when it had become clear they would be leaving for Canada. One worry at a time, one happiness at a time—a chain of happy links. His lungs were clear although he had been smoking for fifteen years, said an unhappy doctor on contract with the Canadian embassy after examining his X-rays. Relief. His teeth perfect. His suitcase sound. His record collection sold as a whole to a passionate collector who would take good care of it. The slides of his works organized. Several of his paintings, verified for export by the Ministry of Culture, rolled up and ready to go. Sara's and his documents translated, the English versions with big red happy stamps on them. Books packed. Clothes packed. A few more books tucked in. Their mothers had been brave at parting—a few tears, some spastic kissing, some words of support. The minibus on time. A decent espresso at the airport. An easy flight to Paris and then on to Toronto. A clean hotel with more stars than it deserved on Charles Street. Silent tears one night while Sara slept next to him—

but that was all right, it was the first cry of a newborn. A promising ad and an agreeable apartment in a highrise on Isabella Street. A trip to IKEA and several hours with a screwdriver and a hammer afterwards. God created the world from prefab. A good shower. An afternoon with paint and now a patio table for two in Yorkville.

It was mid-October, 1993. Ten months into a chapter that started with New Year's Eve.

Boris did not tell Sara about Johnny. What could he have said? That he had seen him, that Johnny had indeed been with the Candyman, that the Candyman had saved Johnny's life by killing two other people, and then had spared the life of Johnny's lover, who was taking a shower in the apartment when Boris visited? No fucking way.

Truth is for those who own it, because they paid its price, they have the cuts, the bruises, the broken bones. His truth, Boris's truth, was that he did not know what to make of Johnny's story. He believed his friend—believed every syllable—but he was not sure if Johnny understood what had happened to him or that it had changed him. All right, he had tried to stay true to himself, but the wall does not choose the colour painted on it.

He wouldn't remain silent about seeing Johnny forever— he owed it to Sara, if nothing else—but stories need the right opening.

When he met her two days before New Year's Eve, she asked him to come with her to a party. Their original plans had revolved around Johnny—he was supposed to play a big New Year's concert—but now everything was in shambles. It turned out to be a theme party. Everyone was dressed in lamé and danced the bump under slivers of light from a disco ball, of which the hostess was especially proud. The props and the music carried the guests back to their teenage years, and the party quickly fell into bad jokes, rude behaviour, and drunken yelling. Sara looked embarrassed most of the evening, and they left right after midnight. In the cab, she told Boris that she wanted to spend a couple of days at her father's cottage on Kopaonik Mountain (her parents had divorced when she was five). By the way she spoke, it was understood that he would go with her. He remembered the night of January 2 now, sitting in Yorkville. He would never forget it.

The snow started falling in the early afternoon, and then it suddenly sped up while the last drifts of light climbed up the pines. In just a few hours, the blizzard had turned the thin, old veil of white into a thick cloud, and then stopped as abruptly as it had started. The two of them had dinner during the storm—Tom Waits singing on a German shortwave radio station—and after it calmed down, they decided to take a walk. When Boris opened the door, a pile of snow fell into the room, covering his feet, and they stood at the doorstep, looking out at the enchanted trees. Their earlier tracks had disappeared, the animal tracks, too: everywhere they looked there was only virgin snow. Slowly, they walked a few yards away from the house to sit on a small snow cloud covering the wooden beam beside the gate. A few scattered lights in the distance glittered like the crystals of memories.

Then Sara said, "Bosnia is in that direction—one war. Croatia's over there—another war. If we hold our breath, we can probably hear the cannons." Boris remained silent. "I know that Johnny was in Belgrade. I went to his apartment yesterday. Your cigarettes were there. Why didn't you tell me?"

He couldn't figure out how to answer.

"You wanted to spare me something. Was he wounded?" Boris shook his head.

"Johnny was with a woman, right?"

Boris held his breath.

"I see."

A mild gust of wind shook some snow off a branch, and it fell in slow motion.

Sara spoke again, very quietly. "I feel as if I have lost my fingers. I cannot hold on to anything. I wish I could sleep through the winter. Have the slow dreams of spring. You wouldn't let me stay out here tonight, by any chance?"

Boris put his arm around her so lightly it almost floated above her shoulders. She stayed as she was, not leaning on him, but not pulling away.

"Where was he going?" she said.

"He wasn't sure. He mentioned Amsterdam."

"Why didn't he call me?"

"He tried. You didn't answer. He had to go. He had deserted."

"Why hasn't he called again?"

"He said he was going to call when he got settled."

"He left with the woman?"

Boris nodded.

She let out a sigh.

"Come with me to Canada," he whispered.

What was he thinking at that moment? Later, in Belgrade, when he replayed the conversation, he persuaded himself that it was an honest proposal. Canada meant distance, meant clean, fresh, balm, healing. Canada was simply an idea. Was that not a good moment to tell her everything about Johnny? She did not ask for more, she could not handle more. You don't hurl the truth at someone in such a frame of mind. And he didn't tell a single lie.

That was how it all started, that was the beginning of this side of the world. The rest was speed, was blur.

They returned to Belgrade with something new between them. They started seeing each other more often, discussing the details of the new life they were planning. One Sunday he realized that they had been together every day that week, and he was not that surprised. What was unexpected, though, was the change in his attitude. He felt better than he had since the war had started, stronger. His focus had shifted from the grey streets around them; they—in their small talk—had already moved to skyscrapers with glorious vistas of Toronto. He liked that he now knew how much sugar went into her espresso, that she knew it was always sparkling, never still water, with his coffee. She knew his favourite jacket, and teased him about it (it was torn on the left shoulder, and roughly patched). He learned that she could not stand watching people biting their nails, and he started biting his occasionally, something he had never done before. They touched often, but that was nothing special—everyone touched everyone in Belgrade. Without talking about it, the café in the bookstore on the Square of the Republic became their favourite place.

One day, Boris offhandedly said that Sara's chances of getting a visa would increase if they were married—fictionally, of course; she laughed, and he did too. They discussed the number of their fictional children. Boris said he had a fictional father. And then, another day, Sara asked him to marry her. And he agreed. They set the wedding for March 7 at noon. There was no reason for a celebration—this was strictly business. It would just be the two of them, their witnesses, and their mothers.

In the second half of February, Boris received a strange phone call. When the unknown male voice asked for him, Boris replied that he did not know Boris Bulic, that he had only recently moved into the apartment. The man asked if Bulic had left a forwarding address, and Boris said no. He offered to take a message, just in case the ex-tenant came by, but the man hung up. Boris was not sure what it was—whether his father wanted to keep him in the country by sending him to the army or if someone was trying to trace Johnny through him—but he stopped answering unexpected phone calls. He warned Sara to do the same. The times are strange and people are mean, he said, and it's healthy to be paranoid. His phone kept ringing at odd times, sometimes early in the morning. Sara reported the same thing, and Boris feared for her safety.

A few days before the wedding, Boris found a message in his mailbox from Johnny's drummer. He read it then threw it away. He would not think about that. The cab was finally cancelled, the lost chance was found again.

The night before the wedding, a freakish cold wave swept over Serbia. In Belgrade, the temperature fell to minus seven, and the snow that had begun to melt turned to ice. Their cab hit another car a few hundred yards from the door, and Boris arrived at his wedding with a bandage covering a cut on his left cheek. Sara's mother fell and broke her finger on the steps outside the registrar's office. In their wedding pictures, they joked later, they looked like a gang who had kidnapped a beautiful woman.

In April, Sara and Boris had an interview at the Canadian embassy, and the official told them they had passed. In late May, they received their papers.

They continued to live separately. Boris sold a few of his works to get some money for their new beginning (minor stuff at humble prices, but everything counted). Sara, in the meantime, went into some sort of slow mode. She did not tell anyone that she was emigrating, except her parents. She wasn't saying goodbye to her friends, she did not want to change anything in her apartment, she just wanted to pack her two suitcases and leave. At times, Boris was afraid that she had changed her mind, but he didn't ask. He knew she was walking a thin wire across an abyss, and he wanted her to keep stepping towards him.

In the summer, two tabloids speculated about Johnny's whereabouts. One of them claimed he was in the U.S., recording his new album with studio musicians. The other one was closer to the truth, in a perverted sort of way: in spite of his being an opponent of the war, Johnny was a true patriot, the article said, and had decided to volunteer on the side of the Bosnian Serbs. Currently, the hero was on leave somewhere abroad, avoiding the local media. In late August, a government-controlled newspaper published a vitriolic commentary about how the times had changed: those who were once considered criminals were now investing their own money and lives in fighting against the Croatian and the Muslim separatists, while those who opposed the war—"the so-called intellectuals"—were in hiding, waiting for the apocalypse to pass, so they could return to earning money from the same people they never cared about. As an example of the first group, the author explicitly mentioned the Candyman and a few other minor gangsters, while in the "so-called" group was Johnny, among others.

Sara never discussed these articles with Boris. She never mentioned Johnny at all. But he did not take this as a sign that she had lost interest in his whereabouts.

Finally, Boris booked the plane tickets from Budapest for October 6. On the evening of Tuesday, October 5, the red minibus peeled off from Slavija Square and, before they had even settled properly in their seats, the lights of Belgrade were behind them. There were four people with them on the bus, silent and teary-eyed. The driver played some disco music, trying to wash their brains, but it did not work.

Their flight arrived early in Paris, and they had time to take the Métro into the city for the afternoon. They walked through the Latin Quarter, dined in a fine restaurant, and went back to the airport hotel when they were already sweetly tired.

The room was so tiny the TV dangled from the ceiling, the reading lamps were on the wall, the coat hanger was suspended above the door. The soundproofing was poor, and every few minutes they heard another plane taking off. It was difficult to fall asleep in their narrow bed. They watched television until after midnight, and Sara fell asleep first. Boris set the alarm, muted the TV, and continued to watch.

He didn't know what time it was when he woke up, but there was still no blue in the sky and the TV was still on. He got up, pressed the power button, and went back to bed. Sara's body sensed his and she shifted towards him. He lay on his side, smelling her hair, her warm ass in his lap, and did not move. His dick rose and stood firm, pulsating against her thigh. He was sure this was a dream. After a while Sara simply put her hand behind her back and took him. He drew his right arm under her body and pulled her closer. Her back arched and he put his left hand on her belly, then slowly slid into her panties. She had shaved on the sides, leaving only a slim strip of hair around her pussy, like a bridge to a better world. It felt like his whole body had narrowed into a shaft. She moaned in her sleep and lazily pulled his foreskin up and down a few times. He touched her and the electricity shook them both. She lifted her left knee to her chin, he moved a little lower and was suddenly in her. Her hips rocked slowly, front and back, far and close, take and give, go and come, come.

Just thinking of it all made him feel as if he were dreaming. But it was Yorkville, they were on a patio, on a sunny October afternoon, far from any winter, and a slim girl in tight black pants was standing next to their table.

"I need an espresso to stir me up," Boris said to the waitress.

"If it's safe to wake up now," Sara said.

Boris suddenly felt that the chain of happy links was finished. The necklace was around his neck and it was surprisingly heavy.

Note: We have to forget

I would love to be able to write something that does not relate to my experience in any way, something completely alien to my thoughts. But memories keep pushing through all the channels, through any channel. If you try to suppress them, they become pimples on your chin, a twitch in your eye, or a cramp in your leg. They bore into you silently, connecting darkness with pain, pain with beauty, beauty with patina, and in the end, betray your writing as a footnote to the things that have happened.

Memories are water in our brain. Without them, it would be dry and boring, but with them, it's dull and unresponsive.

Here is a paradox: As we pile up memories, we become who we are. But memories tend to lie, using the same process as our dreams. Retrospectively, we become better, smarter, gentler, bigger. Everything is justified, valid, an important step to something else. We stabbed because bloodletting saved their lives. We never loved those who left us, we always loved those who helped us. Lie after lie after lie. Are we just a set of lies? A projection made after ironing out our past?

We should forget everything if we want to live. If we want to be, we have to forget.

—T.O., October 18, 1993

MRS. UPSATT. *October 26, 1993*

Although Sara could not relax until she and Boris had some tangible opportunity within their reach, she soon discovered—with surprise—that she enjoyed their first days in Toronto. After mostly empty shelves in Belgrade stores and worried faces in the streets, this place was full of light. Other than where the skyscrapers clustered in the financial district, the sky felt bigger, more generous here. And the low buildings seemed encouraging because they were scalable.

For the first few days they went to bed early, their bodies still on Belgrade time, and woke up at odd hours of the night, making coffee and talking for hours, sometimes even taking a walk on the streets before they started smelling of gas and greed.

Following the map of all immigrants—from furniture stores to dingy dollar stores, from supermarkets to drugstores—they always chose an unknown street. They wanted to keep meeting Toronto. And they wanted to extend their honeymoon, begun on that Paris night.

Boris seemed happy. Something pushed Sara to be more of everything. She was kinder during the day and sluttier during the night, she wanted to make nice food for them, she avoided anything that might be perceived as irritating. At first, she liked this new her, and thought that it must have come from the magic of the blank sheet of paper they suddenly had before them. Or perhaps from having sex again. But she was also confused, because this new woman was pretty much everything the old Sara had never wanted to be. She was too bland, too "if you please."

One day, Sara called her mother, who slipped in another "now that you have left me alone" speech. Buying indulgence, Sara offered a set of comforting lies. Mom, the apartment is unbelievably large (a junior one-bedroom). Boris has enough money so that we can live for a year, even if we don't earn a single cent (in two months, they would be out on the street). We have met some very wealthy people (stepping suddenly onto the street, they were almost killed by an expensive-looking Cadillac; the tinted windows slid down and the driver and his passenger both yelled at them). Those who are dealing out guilt think they rule, but are manipulated in self-defence.

Was she intent on pleasing Boris because she felt guilty? About what?

Two weeks after they arrived, Sara got a job at Mr. Satt's store, selling cameras and video equipment, minimum wage plus commission. She had lied on her résumé, as someone back in Belgrade had told her to do, saying that her father had a photo-equipment store where she'd helped occasionally when not ordering merchandise and doing the bookkeeping. Also, she had lied about her qualifications, claiming to be only a high-school graduate.

Of course she did know something about video cameras and editing units from her years on television, and Mr. Satt was happy with her attitude towards his customers. He was in his late forties, with fair skin and mild manners. There was something vaguely Scandinavian about him, but he never spoke of his background. His accent—not distinct enough to be pinpointed—could be detected only occasionally. He preferred to spend his time alone in the small office on the upper level at the back of the store, where he could scrutinize the main floor through a two-way mirror. The store was on Yonge Street, only two blocks from where they lived, and full of glass and halogen light. There was a room at the back, a tiny studio actually, with a kitchenette, a breakfast table, and even a comfortable couch. Sara brought a few magazines from home, a cheap vase she had found in the garbage on Yonge and filled it with red flowers. She liked to take her breaks there, though nobody else did.

Soon, the Romanian sales clerk, a skinny, dark-haired girl, observed, "You spend too much time in the cage."

"The cage?"

"That's what we call it because that is where Mr. Satt keeps his wife. She is not good in her brain, you know. We call her Mrs. Upsatt."

"I've never seen her. Is she dangerous?"

"I don't think so. She just throws words at you. But she can really make you tired with her stories."

It was her first Saturday, their busiest day. They sold most of their stuff on weekends, since people seemed to need time when buying video cameras. Sometime after five the influx of customers started abating, and Sara went to the kitchenette to make a coffee.

A woman was lying on the couch. She was turned away from the door, gazing into a mirror she had propped against the wall. With one hand, leaning on a pillow, she held back her dark hair. Her back was elongated, and there was some elegance in the way her body filled the space. Although she was dressed, it felt as if she were naked. The late light coming through the small window in the back of the room was the colour of cream. For a second, Sara thought that she was looking at a Velázquez painting, perhaps a vision of Venus, a giant poster someone had put there to make fun of her. Her first reaction was to go in and tear it apart. But there was no Cupid in the picture.

"Close the door, please," the woman said. Only then did Sara notice that she could see the woman's face in the mirror. She closed the door behind her.

"Who are you?"

"Sara."

"You are new."

Sara nodded. "I started on Monday."

"Not in the store. In this country."

The woman sat up, and turned to face her. "Can you pass me those nuts from the shelf, please?"

Sara saw the small plastic bag that had not been there before. She handed it to the woman.

"Thank you." The woman's voice was deep and calm and did not change in pitch as she spoke. "You don't find it funny?"

"What?" Sara said.

"That a nut asks for nuts. It is almost like being a cannibal." She stared at Sara. When Sara did not react, she said, slowly, "Do you understand what I am saying?"

"Perfectly well. I don't see what's funny."

"Hmm." She tore the bag open and started picking out nuts one by one, with two fingers only, watching Sara's face all the time.

Sara started to feel annoyed, but refused to show it. "I wanted to make myself a coffee. Would you like some?"

"No. I can't drink coffee. But you go ahead. What is your name?"

"Sara."

"You don't look Jewish."

"I'm not. I'm Yugoslav."

"Then you must be a Serb. Sara the Serb."

"How did you know?"

"Mr. Satt says that only Serbs say they come from Yugoslavia. Everyone else says their nationality."

Sara stood motionless by the coffeemaker.

"I didn't want to offend you, Sara," the woman said.

"I'm not offended. Is it true what you said? Is that really so?"

"I don't know. I don't meet many people. Ask Mr. Satt." The woman stood up and put the bag with the nuts on the table. "I am Luz. Let me make the coffee."

NIGHT IDENTITIES. *October 31, 1993*

It was their first Halloween ever—there was no such holiday in Yugoslavia. Boris asked the man in the German delicatessen on Church Street about it, the only person he knew in Toronto besides Sara. The man enjoyed explaining the rituals of the night to a newcomer, and then sold Boris a bag of mixed candies, which he hung on the inside of the door to their apartment. Their building—a block away from the gay village, and large enough for individual tenants to go unnoticed—was full of transvestites, prostitutes, junkies, dealers, and gay couples. But the kids still might come, the man had said.

Sara returned from her job early that afternoon. Another girl had come to work by mistake, so Sara took pity on her and gave her the shift. She took a shower while Boris made dinner. They sat at the table and watched the world news on their small TV as they ate. The food was good. In the liquor store Boris had picked up a free magazine that had some recipes. This one was supposedly from Bosnia.

"Do you think this is some kind of solidarity?" Sara asked. "That they want so badly to be in sync with the news that they called this Bosnian?"

"Irritating, isn't it? We ran away as far as we could, and politics is still infiltrating our food."

"But look: it contains ingredients that were never available back home."

Boris said, "I remember once passing by a restaurant in Amsterdam that claimed to have authentic Serbian cuisine. The dessert was something made of anise and whipped cream and avocados, country style."

"Right. Just something that your typical Serbian peasant would make at the end of a hard day—whipped cream on top of avocados. And anise?"

"What is that?" Boris said.

He was not talking about the ingredient. He was trying to hear the sound seeping through the door. Sara, too, now heard laughter in the corridor. But there was no knocking at their door. Boris waved his hand and poured some wine.

"I read an article this morning in the *Star*," Boris said. "It said that inflation in Belgrade is now over seventy million per cent."

"You were in the library?"

"I was trying to find something about arts funding in Canada. There's a book about it, but it was out, so I took something about writing résumés."

"Why would you need advice—?"

Sounds in the corridor again. Boris went to the door, looked through the peephole, then returned to his chair.

"They recommend one page if possible, two maximum."

They now ate in silence. The footsteps in the corridor came and went, muffled by the sound of the news. There was no knocking at the door. A short report about the siege of Sarajevo.

"What do they think they're doing?" Sara said.

"Maybe we should put a pumpkin in front of our door," Boris said.

"What is the purpose of cutting people off?"

"Of course, they don't know that we want them to visit."

A loud commercial came on and Boris stood up to find the remote. He zapped until he found a *Seinfeld* repeat. Sara removed her plate, took a bunch of grapes, and sat on the sofa, folding her legs to the side. Boris rummaged through the fridge.

"What are you looking for?" she said, picking at the grapes.

"I'm trying to find something that we might use instead of a pumpkin. You haven't heard of anything, have you?"

"No, the girls at work are mostly immigrants, they don't know much about Halloween either."

Boris came and sat next to her. He decided to light a cigarette and stood up again to get the ashtray. On his way back, he checked the peephole. When the commercials came on again, Boris muted the TV.

"Strange how I find this show funny, but not to laugh out loud," Sara said.

"Then it isn't funny," Boris said.

"No, it is. But I am laughing on the inside."

"You mean you're laughing at internal jokes?"

"No, inside me. Don't you have that? Laughing inside?"

"Oh. Yes, with Woody Allen."

"See."

They watched in silence as father and son fought over a hamburger. A dog appeared behind a garage and stole the food. *Seinfeld* came back on and Boris hit the sound button.

Around ten, he said, "Let's go to Church Street—they have some sort of carnival."

In the elevator with them were a skeleton, a Hun, two porno nuns, and something that could have been a woman or a man, wearing an enormous dildo and two rubber breasts the size of watermelons, with long hair that looked natural and large hands tattooed with Portuguese.

By unspoken agreement they sat on the wooden bench next to the entrance to see who else came out. Boris lit a cigarette and jokingly offered it to Sara. She took it.

"Aren't people supposed to start smoking when they're nervous?" he said.

"Probably."

"Are you nervous?"

"I feel good, B. If I smoke it now, I won't get hooked."

Boris hugged her, smiling.

Out the front door came a group of sexy female pirates, a shapely leg protruding through the cloak on one, bare arms on another, a very low cut jacket on the third. They laughed and hugged as they turned right towards Church Street. Almost immediately afterwards came a few Brazilian transvestites dressed like sylphs. A staccato of giggling as they followed the first group. A Roman soldier came next, then Robin Hood and his Merry Men with corn and sausages in their pants, then a nun who wore a cross made of two large phalluses. All of them were laughing, everyone hurrying to get to Church, to find their company, to model their night identities.

"Let's dress up as Canadians and go," Boris said.

He felt Sara's shoulders tremble almost imperceptibly. By the light of the street lamp above them he saw that her cheeks were shiny. He opened his mouth to ask, then changed his mind, and hugged her tight.

"But I'm laughing on the inside," Sara said.

Note: Face

My face is a good face. It never betrays me. It lets me sit comfortably behind it and does not call for me unless it's necessary. It is made of elastic material that is resistant to most atmospheric influences. My face can take an insult, an injury, and it will repair itself and be like new again.

I can wash it, shave it, slap it, pinch it, steam it, wipe it, I can even cut it, and it will still be my face. I am not sure how, but people recognize me by my face. It keeps changing, but they can still distinguish me by it. I've had three different moustaches, and five different beards, and I was still me. I've plucked my eyebrows, I've shaved my sideburns and trimmed my hair, and yet still people know me.

There is nothing different from anyone else about my face. Two eyes, two eyebrows, a nose, a mouth, and cheeks—everyone has the same things. When I make a face, it is anyone's expression. It is the same pattern repeated five billion times all over the globe, yet humans are capable of recognizing a particular pattern as a person's private mould. Maybe that is what makes us unique as a species—not language, not history, not religion, but our ability to recognize faces.

That's why we invented masks.

—T.O., November 3, 1993

THE SAME SILENT MUSIC. *November 9, 1993*

Sara was supposed to come home that day around two, and Boris decided to take a walk to his favourite delicatessen and get something nice for lunch.

He came to the corner of Isabella and Church, then, on a whim, crossed Church Street, walked a few blocks east, then south on Sherbourne, and returned by Wellesley Street to the store. It was a Friday, cold but sunny, and he felt a glow envelop him, making him light and bearable. Watching gay couples around him walking hand in hand, something unimaginable where he came from, he suddenly felt that he really had crossed the ocean, that he had arrived—whatever that meant—and he could hardly wait to share this feeling with Sara.

He bought a bag of groceries, and took the long way back home. Instead of going north, towards his street, he walked west, towards Yonge.

If he told someone in Belgrade that he was elated by watching men holding hands on the streets, they would think he had become gay. If he wrote a letter, now, to a friend back there, what would he write? He realized it would have to be a group of scenes, not a narrative. A scene of their first encounter with the city. A scene in IKEA. Another in a huge supermarket. A Yorkville scene. The Halloween scene, which was maybe even an act. All written as a movie script. Exterior. Day. Busy corner in an upscale neighbourhood. Interior. Night. Thoughts flapping in all directions, searching for ways to keep his head above water.

There is no narrative of exile. There are poems of exile, long successions of short verses, plenty of metaphors, abbreviations, aberrations, abeyances. Exile is not transferable. It is a chopped-up existence. Exiles live their days as a series of small coloured stones whose final order is never fully revealed to them. The mosaic they create in the end will be visible only to their descendants.

Against the wall of a clothing boutique, a rectangular bundle of paper caught his attention. He picked it up. He was still not entirely familiar with Canadian banknotes, but it does not take much to recognize money on the street.

Judging by the colour, these banknotes were not small denominations. To his surprise, he was not happy. Why did it have to be him to find the money when so many people had passed by? Because he kept staring at the sidewalk in front of him like an old man. Immigrants and the old: exiles from life. Frail, vulnerable, futureless. All his life he had looked people straight in the eyes, but here he had suddenly stopped. You don't have to carry hellos with you. But hellos are anchors. They keep you glued to the ground. With nobody who was familiar to greet, he had cut off all eye contact, hacking through faces straight to the asphalt beneath him. The asphalt was the same in Belgrade, Amsterdam, London, Prague, Barcelona. Sometimes more spittle, sometimes less, sometimes more trash, sometimes less ammonia—it was the same map of the same dance steps. The same silent music.

This was his present—when you do not look at faces but at sidewalks, when you are searching for a recognizable sound, when people are around you but you are not among them. This was why he was excited about finding the money, but not happy.

He went into a store that sold art materials to buy a few sheets of drawing paper. At the cashier, he took out the money and unfolded it. Three bills of twenty dollars each. He paid, took his paper, and walked out. As he was putting the money back in his pocket, he let a fiver fall on the sidewalk. He crossed the street to a coffee shop, bought himself an espresso, and found a chair in the window facing the art store.

After almost an hour, a man picked up the money. Boris hurried after him.

"Excuse me, do you have a minute? I saw you find that money, and I thought you must be a newcomer like me, and—"

"Fuck off, faggot," the man said, raising his middle finger.

TWINS. *November 16, 1993*

Sara stood by the store window, looking out. It was Tuesday, mid-November. The air was crisp. The low sun shone on the buildings across the street, and Yonge was already filling up with the rush-hour crowd, although it was only several minutes past three. Tucked away behind several cameras on display and cardboard ads for new models, she was studying the faces of the passersby. From time to time she recognized Slavic features, and a few people, she thought, might even be Serbs.

A customer entered, but she judged him to be a browser and let another clerk take over. She had already sold a few expensive cameras that afternoon, mostly to American tourists, and she was content with her earnings for the day.

The man left and the two other clerks started chatting. Sara continued to watch the street. One or two faces, she thought, were types easily found here and everywhere, but some were not. She remembered the doppelgänger legend, but that was too ominous, too scary for her taste. This was something else: perhaps everyone had their twin some-where far away, and between them there was a balance of pleasure, an equilibrium of success, of riches, of health. Sitting on the same see-saw, on opposite sides of the world, the twins go up and down, down and up, one feeling good, the other one miserable with the flu, one struggling to buy food, the other renovating a villa in Tuscany. One losing a loved one, the other discovering that she is pregnant. With someone who was never there, a total stranger, past before ever becoming present.

Luz entered the store like a moving shadow, in a long black coat, a dark hat, and black boots. She nodded to the other girls, who nodded back, and went straight upstairs to her husband's office. Sara left her position by the window and went to the cage. She filled the electric kettle with fresh water and pressed the button.

Luz came in.

"Are you in here all the time, or do you work sometimes?"

"I'm making you some tea," Sara said.

Luz took off her coat and hat and threw them towards the coat rack in the corner. She missed and they ended up in a heap on the floor. Sara hung them up. When she turned around, Luz was on the couch, her hands covering her face. Sara poured the tea into two cups and sat by Luz, holding them. For a minute or two, nothing happened. Then, slowly, Luz extended her hand and took a cup. She did not try to hide the tears.

"Not a good day?"

They drank tea in silence.

"What happened?"

"I went to the doctor. He increased my dose."

Silence, again.

"Have you ever fainted?" Luz asked.

"Once, when I was sixteen. I forgot to have breakfast. And lunch. I was in love."

"Did the world spin around you?"

"It did. It went fast."

"You are lucky, then. It never spun around me. I was always in the wrong place, never in the centre. I am a moon, Sara. I orbit this world. When you find me on the couch, that's what it is: I will fall off if I do not lie down."

Pause.

"How long have you been here?" Sara asked.

"Sixteen years. Some people emigrate and are fine in a year, some are never fine. You don't fit. You're bent and the new space was made for straight, for upright."

"I feel bent," Sara said.

"All new immigrants do. Look at them. They have fear in their eyes. They are trying to keep their balance. They think they will fall if they straighten up. Even when they faint, the world does not revolve around them."

Luz started crying again in complete silence, without sobbing, without sighs, without covering her face. Sara put her cup on the floor and hugged her without thinking.

She is an expert at crying, Sara thought. A tear rolled down Sara's cheek, too, stealthily. Another followed. Is she crying because of Luz? Impossible. Another tear.

"Are you afraid of returning home?" Luz asked quietly.

"I just came here, I'm not even thinking about returning."

"That fear—that is your prison. Once you emigrate, you start thinking that returning home would mean defeat. But if you become locked inside that, you will accept anything that life throws your way."

"When you fly across half the world," Sara said, "you expect your troubles to stay behind to dry up and die. But they arrive before you, they make your bed, they await you in your mirror."

"I used to be a writer back in Brazil," Luz said. "I published two books before I came to Canada. Two good books. And then my mind just snapped. As if the move was just too much. You know—when too much happens to you, you can't write anymore. Your drain is plugged—your dirty water is drowning you. If I don't take my pills, I have horrible visions. People are dying in my head, my closest friends, people are being disfigured, I do it to them. I can't write about what I see, Sara, because I don't want to pass it on to anyone. And I can't go back to Brazil like this. It would feel like a defeat."

The two women sat on the couch, crying. Their breathing soon became coordinated, and had someone blind entered the room, he would have thought that there was only one person inside.

Note: Two shadows from one light
There was a party in Belgrade a long time ago. The hostess invited a woman who read tarot. I don't like that stuff, so I avoided sitting at the table across from her as long as I could. In the end, it became obvious to me that the hostess would take it personally if I did not take part in her plan, so I took a drink with me and sat down.

"I see you walking with two shadows from the same light," the tarot reader told me.

That sentence has been drilling into my brain ever since. Now I know what she meant. My shadows have names.

—T.O., December 29, 1993

ASKA AND WOLF. *May 10, 1994*

Boris had never written his résumé because he had never applied for a job. A résumé was a dry, precise form, tailored for engineers, not artists, on which he was to list his previous engagements, in descending order, his education, also going backwards, his goals and his general qualities. He tried but did not want to fit everything on one page. His life seemed too small on a single sheet. It scared him.

He was tempted to drift into fiction. Who would know? Who would be the witness? Isn't that the purpose of emigration? He could reinvent himself and he could round off the edges a bit, fill in the gaps, paint the walls that life had built around him. Some writers do it. Spies do it all the time. What do they call it—creating a legend? Precisely. He was an artist. Fiction was his legitimate tool.

But when he printed a version that he'd invented and the strictness of the paper replaced the fluidity of the screen, he was disgusted. Not with the lies but with what the lies meant. Uprooted, he had to fight hard for his past, for every memento, every picture, for every treasured moment. The lies blurred his life, corroded reality, let rust take over, made everything the colour of shit.

He wiped his résumé clean of all inventions.

The man was reading Boris's résumé, printed on a yellowish cotton paper as had been recommended in the library book. Boris fought the urge to explain what he meant by each paragraph, and kept silent. They were sitting in a café at Yonge and Bloor. A blond Russian waitress with a low-cut blouse brought them their espressos. The man studying his résumé was in his early forties, apparently in casual clothes. But the longer Boris looked at him, the more he realized how carefully he had dressed. His shirt exactly matched his blue eyes; the signet ring on his right pinkie and his watch were silver. He wore jeans, but the material suggested an expensive designer.

The man laughed. "This is a perfect résumé if the job was to join a revolutionary cell in South America."

Of course. Who would give a job to someone who spent his life doing conceptual art?

"How come they didn't arrest you? Man, this is awesome. You glued your president's picture to a papier-mâché dick. What for?"

"So people could admire and bow to their idol."

"That would never work here. Our prime minister is very tall. It would take too much paper, wipe out a minor rainforest." The man emptied a pouch of brown sugar into his cup and stirred it, looking at Boris. "Have you ever worked in advertising?"

"Lately, all our political work in Belgrade might as well have been a form of advertising," Boris said.

"Sure, sure," the man said.

Boris was desperately trying to remember his name. Chris? Bill? Richard? Dan? He had introduced himself when they met at his office on the twenty-ninth floor of the building towering above them, but Boris was bad with names.

"And this," said the man, slapping the paper in his hand, "the musical gallows, that's great."

Boris felt awkward. The man stopped laughing, took a sip of coffee, said, "I think we could find something for you," then looked briefly at the top corner of the résumé before adding, "Boris."

Boris could not believe it. "That would be great."

"Of course, you don't have Canadian experience— you've been here, what, only three months? But we could prolong the probation period, and that would cover us."

The man pursed his lips. "How about this: you get a position as a senior graphic designer. That would practically mean you could work as an art director, since you would have junior people to execute the design for you, and it wouldn't draw too much attention to your background. After the probation period is over—say, in a year—we would drag you one floor up, pair you with a writer, and give you a proper title. Now, the tricky part is your salary. What did you have in mind?"

Boris had read about this moment, but he still was not ready.

"Come on, Boris, don't be shy," the man urged.

"I was thinking thirty . . . five," Boris said quietly.

"Thirty-five," the man repeated slowly. "Yeah, I think we can live with that. So, can you start this Monday?"

"Yes."

"Good. Welcome aboard, Boris. You will love our agency, you'll see. It's not for nothing that ODG operates on five continents and is looking for the sixth." He laughed at his own joke and stood up, extending his hand. "Pleasure, Boris."

"Thank you . . ."

The man smiled. "Johnny. You can call me Johnny, Boris."
Boris squeezed his hand hard.

For the first few weeks, Boris had to learn so many things
that his mind was numb by the end of the day. The proper
use of a workstation, how to file new material, procedures
(explained by those who had offices) and ways to circum-
vent them (explained by those in cubicles), the company
infrastructure, the history of specific clients, and names,
names, names. For the most part, his co-workers were
friendly, but he did not want to test their patience and tried
learning as much as he could by watching them, rather than
asking. Many of them wanted to know more about the war
in his old country, and he always answered with as much
detail as he judged would not bore the listener.

He slowly fell into the space opened for him and he was
given some serious projects. He took Sara to an exclusive
restaurant on Yorkville Avenue for a celebratory dinner. All
was going well, except for the pattern of terrible headaches
that had developed during his seventh week.

He would get to work at nine, carry on with the design
of the current project, answer some phone calls and his
email, talk to the colleagues in the cubicles next to his or
just listen to their chatter—it was all interesting. Around
lunchtime, a throbbing just behind his forehead announced
the arrival of the pain that soon hit his temples with brutal force and stayed there until evening. He tried the first
line of painkillers, then those marked extra-strength,
without success. His doctor, an older woman who made a
big fuss about his smoking, finally agreed to prescribe

something with codeine, and that worked. But the pills were mildly hallucinogenic, and he couldn't continue to work drugged and constipated. He put off taking his pills till the end of the day.

Sara had found some books in Serbian in the back of a bin in a second-hand bookstore on Yonge, and one day he took an old paperback, written by Ivo Andrić, a Serbian Nobel laureate, with him to work. Among the collection of stories was Boris's favourite allegory, "Aska and Wolf," about a lamb who could dance beautifully. One day, Aska the lamb gets lost in the forest and meets a big bad wolf who is clearly planning to eat her. Aska starts dancing to say goodbye to this world, and the wolf becomes entranced and keeps postponing the kill. She dances long enough for the shepherds to come and save her, surviving only because of her art.

That day, his head already throbbing, he took the book with him to lunch two blocks away, at a small restaurant hidden behind a building on a side street where his colleagues rarely went. The owner and his wife, a Middle Eastern couple, were the only employees. She cooked all the food—mostly Italian dishes—and he served and worked at the counter. Boris took his ravioli to the small smoking section in the back and opened his book.

An hour later, after an espresso and three cigarettes, his headache was gone.

He repeated everything the next day, with the same result. Wanting to find out what in that ritual had cured him, Boris tried eliminating ingredients. He changed restaurants, ate different food, tried tea instead of coffee, did not eat at all, but the headaches still vanished after lunch. Sure that it was the writer's magic, he brought another book from the same batch with him, but the throbbing still stopped. Certain that he was cured of whatever it was that he had, he brought *The New Yorker* with him to read during lunch. His head exploded again.

He finally figured it out: the shelter of his mother tongue had cured him.

Note: Lucifer
No wonder some people are afraid of immigrants. Back where we came from, we were in the light—the light of our language, of our own culture, in our own heaven—and then we fell out of it. We are all Lucifers. The fear of immigrants is a biblical fear.

—*T.O., June* 11, 1994

MIRROR. *May 24, 1995*

It was a glorious May morning, bright, warm, and not too humid, which was a small miracle considering that there had been a heavy downpour all night long. Sara had finished her article around two in the morning, woke up around eight to take another look at it, made a few changes, and took the printout to the *NOW Magazine* offices on the Danforth. Her editor read it while she sat at his desk. It was all good to go. Happy, Sara decided to take a little break. She took the subway to Yonge and Bloor and walked to her old workplace.

Sara wanted to take Luz to Yorkville, and Luz said she didn't mind as long as they went there through the underground city. When they left the store together, the clerks looked like they had seen a ghost. They walked one block west and went downstairs by Mr. Grocer, where they entered the corridors full of stores under the Manulife Centre. Five minutes later, they resurfaced at Bellair and Cumberland. Sara led Luz across the street and through the short passage to the Coffee Mill. The small, secluded patio was full, so they went inside and sat in the far corner, by the glass wall. Except for two old Hungarian ladies, they were alone.

"I read your articles," Luz said. "You are angry at your old country."

A middle-aged Hungarian woman came to take their order. Sara asked for two chestnut purées.

"I guess I am," she said when the waitress left, "but not because I miss it, if that's what you mean."

"No. But people think they have left voluntarily when they were actually squeezed out. You have every right to be angry, but I didn't expect that it would last this long."

Sara leaned her forehead on her hand and looked outside. "It's been a year and a half," she finally said. "It's not that long."

Luz nodded.

After Boris got his job in advertising, Sara was able to quit the store to find something better. She saw an ad in the gay village weekly, had an interview, but their enthusiasm cooled when she mentioned her husband. The people at *NOW* were much more open, and she got her first opportunity only a week after she had called: they asked her to cover a conference on Yugoslavia being held at the University of Toronto. After five days of sitting in the auditorium at Innis College listening to academics, politicos, and self-proclaimed experts from her old country arguing, Sara knew: there was no going back. The wound was full of pus. It would take years to heal, maybe decades. For the first time since she had come to Canada, she felt good about leaving.

Five days later, her article appeared. They gave it a plug on the cover and two full pages inside. She felt better than she had expected. Actually, she felt happy. From that point on, she published on average one article every other week, and—although the money wasn't good enough to live on—she had found again a big piece of her identity.

The woman brought their desserts.

"So, what are you going to do now?"

"I've enrolled in an M.A. program at Ryerson. Media production. I have enough experience from Belgrade to do it relatively easily."

"How is your husband?"

"He's good, I guess. I haven't seen much of him lately. He's working on another big campaign."

Luz circled her spoon in her chestnut purée, eroding the food symmetrically rather than eating it.

"How are you?" Sara asked.

"Better. Are you two good?" Luz asked without looking up.

"Why do you ask?"

"Then you're not."

"Luz."

Another half-circle around the centre. Silence. Sara's sigh. A few random spoonfuls of purée. The other half of the circle. Sara signalled with her hand, and the waitress came. She ordered an espresso and some sparkling water for Luz.

"No, we're good. It's just . . . I don't know why I'm telling you this."

"Because you can."

"I feel guilty."

"Guilty?"

"Boris has done so much for us, right from the start. He opened up my eyes about Canada, he got the papers, he arranged our wedding, he earned the money for us to start here. I just don't know if I'm giving enough back to him."

"Sometimes just being there is enough," Luz said.

"We don't argue. We support each other. And there is a feeling that probably has its name in some language, but it isn't love. Not on my part. I've never told you how Boris and I met. I was in love with his best friend."

There was no change in Luz's expression.

"My boyfriend disappeared. He was sent to fight, and I never heard from him again. I know he's not dead, I just know, but he never tried to find me. What was I supposed to do?"

The waitress appeared with their drinks and took away the empty purée dishes. Luz remained silent.

"I know, you're going to ask me why I married Boris—"

"Not at all. That's a stupid question. In fact, I won't ask you anything. All the questions and all the answers are yours. I think you need a mirror." She coughed into her hand and drank a little water.

"A miracle?"

"A mirror," Luz repeated. "Everyone needs a mirror. Not a piece of glass, dear. But the people around you. Your people. You have lost your country, your language, your place. You have no refuge. There is no reflection of you. You must find something to measure yourself with. Not against. With. Either you let yourself go, give yourself to the wind, and see where it takes you . . ."

"Or?"

"Or you find a mirror in something, someone."

Sara stared into her dark eyes, but Luz did not show any sign that she would continue to talk.

Sara sighed. "I don't know how to do any of that."

Note: Sunglasses

You can search for the perfect sunglasses all your life. First, they have to suit your face, make you look mysterious, but not like a spy, hide bushy eyebrows if you have them, and reveal your cheekbones, the only part of the face that looks good even in old age. Then, they have to fit properly, the arms hugging your ears and not turning them into antennae. They should have hydrophilic socks. The nose pads have to be tight, but soft, and not cause sneezing. A guy spent months and thousands of dollars on curing his recent case of sinusitis, taking so many antihistamines and other allergy medicines that his liver became swollen. In the end, he replaced his supermarket shades and was good again. Except for his liver, which could have been sold as foie gras to a restaurant in Coventry.

The lenses are an entirely different story. What do they block? UVA or UVB or UVC or all of them? What about harmful blue light? *Are they impact resistant? Plastic or glass? Is there an iridium coating? Sometimes it's good if the contrast is increased, but sometimes you don't want that. The same lenses can turn a patch of snow into a Tabriz rug, but they can darken your golf course to the point where you will think you are up shit creek. What do you want to see through them? What do you need to hide? Sunglasses are very good at mitigating guilt. If the lenses are dark enough, there will be less contrast between the people around you—they will all turn into one large organism, a faceless, mute presence. It's easier to feel guilt before God than before a crowd.*

It was written somewhere that Nero watched gladiatorial combat through precious stones to dim the sun. He preferred emeralds, they say. Green is the colour of spring, of new life. He was a very ironic man, Nero. You watch men fighting to death, but put a filter between the scene and your eyes, and that filter says, "Death is new life." Perhaps that's why he torched Rome—maybe from his perspective he was giving the city new life. The ultimate catharsis. And it is true: every time you create something new, you kill something old.

The question is whether something new is always born when something old dies. I believe it is. I believe there can be no vacuum of ideas, no emptiness of any kind, anywhere. We don't always see everything, but there is always something there. Energy, matter, rays, colours, feelings, ideas. The planes and ships that disappeared in the Bermuda Triangle—maybe they hit a giant idea that's been floating there for centuries, waiting for the right head.

But green, green over red! A gladiator lashes, and blood spurts, and the crowd is beside themselves—their man has scored. Red is all over the victim. Red excites, inflames. Only one man does not see red; through his emerald, Nero sees dark brown. He is watching the rust taking over a man. The man is corroding before his eyes. While everyone else is enjoying a murder, Nero is being served a metaphor.

Nero didn't go down in history as the man who invented sunglasses, though. That happened in the twelfth century in China. The Chinese took quartz full of imperfections and made metal frames for it, not to protect the eyes from the sun but to make their expression unreadable. The rulers wanted to remain detached from the events and stories before them. They needed cool. They found that looking cool helped them rule. A cold face and hidden eyes will win every time. Emotional people don't get respect.

Still, sunglasses didn't catch on. For eight hundred years nothing much happened. Then came Hollywood. Big stars, bright studio lights, California sunshine, the need to remain beautiful if you wanted to work. Actors adopted sunglasses first. By the 1930s, they really took off. The Polaroid filters of 1936 were the first real protection for the eyes. In World War II, some soldiers got sunglasses sent from home to save their lives in the sunny countries.

I'm still thinking of the way it all started: how the need to protect the eyes conveniently led to the chance to hide the feelings. It was never really about the sun. From the beginning, sunglasses were about hiding oneself from others and cushioning others in our view. They are a Walkman for our eyes.

I bought my first Walkman in 1980, I think only one year after they were invented. It came with a blue holster made of cheap plastic, and I carried it everywhere. In Belgrade, people on the street would look at my headphones, they would follow the cable down to my belt and the strange machine, and—although they did not know what the little box was—they quickly realized it was something that separated me from them. It was great to watch their eyes and their process of deduction. In the end, their eyes would try to meet my eyes, which was, I'm sorry, impossible, because I was wearing dark sunglasses. Their inspection of me invariably ended with a degree of hatred. They thought they were smart and good-looking, and I had no right to filter them out.

At one point, I was almost persuaded that they were right. Too much isolation can thin you out. I bought a small red Aiwa unit that could record as well as play. I would plug in an unobtrusive stereo microphone, walk down the street at noon, and record for as long as the cassette ran. Then I would rewind the tape, take the microphone out and plug the headphones in, and I would continue to walk, listening to the immediate past. I soon discovered that the sounds that other people had just left fitted with those who were just passing me by. It was a resident stream, the native sound of that particular place. You can record a sixty-minute tape on any given street in the world, and then for several years you need not bother listening to the reality of the same place. Even if something dramatic happens, a war starts in that country, a mass murder is committed the previous day, even then—just speed up the tape about five per cent and play it ten per cent louder. That is humankind.

That is why art works.

We are only repeating the words of those who came before us. We are a tape, a very long tape, lasting decades. Sometimes, our words coincide with what is going on around us and what we are saying sounds relevant and fresh.

That is why art works only rarely.

—T.O., June 18, 1996

CITIZENSHIP. *November 29, 1996*

The room was already full of people when they arrived, and Sara and Boris had to ask a woman to remove her bags from two adjacent chairs so they could sit. The space was a large office with a row of numbered windows on one side, its ugliness only emphasized by the cosmetics of red flowers and small paper flags. The amount of red and white, the manner in which someone had decorated this unpleasant space with precision instead of joy, reminded Sara of the Communist holidays of Yugoslavia in her childhood. November 29 was, incidentally, the biggest holiday of the old country, the Day of the Republic, and they still officially celebrated it in Belgrade. The only thing missing here was some revolutionary music and then the Central Committee could enter.

The door on the left suddenly opened and a giant black man in the red uniform of the Royal Canadian Mounted Police led a line of men and women into the room. He told everyone to rise, and then introduced the woman in the middle as the citizenship judge who would preside over the ceremony.

"She's a Tito," Boris whispered.

The judge welcomed everyone and explained in a soft and authoritative voice what was expected of them. Then she read the oath, slowly, and they all repeated after her: "I swear that I will be faithful and bear true allegiance to Her Majesty Queen Elizabeth the Second, Queen of Canada, Her Heirs and Successors, and that I will faithfully observe the laws of Canada and fulfil my duties as a Canadian citizen."

The judge indicated to them to sit and gave a short welcome speech. Sara's mind drifted away. It was her thirtieth birthday the next day, and the symbolism of this event just made it harder to separate things. Was this a new beginning or the pompous end of something? They'd crossed into another life and the door had closed behind them. But what had remained the same, and what had changed?

"What now?" Sara said when they were outside.

"Let's go somewhere for a coffee," Boris said, pulling his collar close to his chin to keep the cold out.

"Sure. But I mean, what now, are we different?"

"Well, yeah, I guess. We're free again."

While slowly walking up Yonge Street, Sara thought about that. She didn't think Boris was being philosophical. He probably meant it on a practical level: they were free again to move, to travel. When the West imposed sanctions against Serbia, their passports had become useless overnight. Not that they had the money to travel, but the fact that they had been at the mercy of the foreign embassies, almost none of which gave visas to Serbs, made them feel locked out and cut off. The Canadian passport was like the Yugoslav one in its glory days: when you had one, only a few countries demanded visas. In that sense, yes, they were free again.

But where to go, what to carry, where to arrive?

Her grandmother, the wife of an army officer, had never worked a day in her life. She was lucky that her husband had chosen the right side when the Germans invaded, and after the war she was awarded a hero's pension. Ever since Sara could remember, her grandmother had always behaved erratically. An image of virtue one day, all shyness and tact and manners; an evil machine the next, torturing Sara's mom and her two other children, demanding, never satisfied. Until she reached her old age, when she became stable in what could best be described as absolute irresponsibility. She just chirped around, light as a feather, nothing touching her, nothing worrying her, as if her life had reached a level of unprecedented ease. As if she could make anything out of it, on a whim turn it into what was only in her dreams.

Once, Sara's mom had reprimanded the old bird. Sara's parents were already divorced and her mom had some worries at work. When she tried to complain to her mother, during their regular daily visit when they brought milk and bread and magazines, Grandma did not even try offering advice, or words of comfort.

"Can you for once try to help me, Mom?" Sara's mother said.

"Darling, it's your life," the old woman had answered. "Nobody can decide for you, right? My life is over now, every day is a bonus, and I just can't be bothered with problems."

As if life were a ride, and when she had arrived at her destination, she had switched the engine off to take a rest.

Had Sara arrived anywhere safe enough to turn the engine off? Had this thing today made a difference?

Note: Dying means forgetting words
If the idealists are right, nothing exists until we name it. Dying, then, must mean forgetting words, losing language, going to the place where there are only shifting shadows and shapeless fogs. Some religions call that place Hell.

Apparently, some people, when they cross that border between life and death, are capable of taking words with them, of keeping the words. When they enter that grey zone, they start naming things, giving birth to colours, passion, energy. They start building a world that is immensely more beautiful than the caricature we live in. Those people go to that world every day, they die a little every day—because that is the only way to enter—and they work, they build, they create, they beautify, hoping that that other world will spill over into this one, and improve it a little.

Some religions call that world Art.

—T.O., September 6, 1997

BEFORE AND AFTER. *June 23, 1998*

Boris had brought an old Pentax with him, its body made of steel, heavy as hell; she used to grumble about having to carry it when his hands were full of cheap furniture, or groceries. There must be some photos from their early days in Canada. She thought they were probably in a box in the closet, waiting in ambush, the way all memories do, but she couldn't recall seeing any, ever.

NOW wanted an article about her immigrant experience, to publish in the Canada Day issue. July 1 was just a week away, and they needed it yesterday. Their art director envisioned a "before and after" sort of thing—one photo from before she knew what was in store for her, and one fresh, now that she knew how generous the store had been.

She rummaged through their closet, and just when she was about to call Boris at work, she found their pictures in the large cardboard box their printer had come in. She was surprised to find them there—the last time she checked they were in a shoebox, as all normal pictures are.

She made a coffee, sat on the floor next to the box, and started taking handfuls of pictures out. At first she flipped through them quickly, trying to stick to her purpose. She liked the art director's idea, and envisioned a picture of herself confused and oddly dressed next to a snapshot of her now. The first handfuls were all of something she wasn't looking for. But then she slowed down. With surprise, she soon realized that although she could remember the general details about where and when each picture had been taken, the minutiae were lost to her. Almost every image was a revelation. Using pictures as doors was fine: she was able to open them, look behind them, see who and what was there, hear the sounds, retrieve the smells—but the doors closed again as soon as she put the picture back in the box.

If you want to forget something, take a picture of it. It's as if the brain, at the moment when the shutter is pressed, gives up its responsibilities and leaves the task of remembering to the emulsion on the film.

Niagara Falls in the background. The three of them are standing by the stone wall. Sara is on the left, all in black—black leather jacket, black jeans, existentialist turtleneck. Boris in the middle, legs wide apart, hands in pockets. In a fighting mood. The man on the right—he was the reason they went there. He is not handsome, but there is a sense of confidence in the way he fills the space. He is posing nonchalantly, his right elbow on the wall, his long hair revealing his profile.

He was an old friend from Fine Arts. He and Boris had once worked together. He had moved to New York some time after Sara and Boris had left Belgrade. He was doing well in Manhattan, had his gallery, and was just preparing a new exhibition. Oils. Perhaps that was why Boris looked so aggressive in the picture. "He sold out," Boris said after the friend was gone. "He's painting now because he can't sell his installations."

When was this photo taken? About a year ago? More—it must have been the early spring of 1997. A young Asian woman had been passing by, alone, and they asked her to take the shot. Then they invited her to join them for a coffee across the road, on the patio. The picture is sunny, but as soon as they sat, the clouds had moved in from the south, and the wind became unpleasant. "Heavy industrial wind, shears like steel. Must be from Detroit," Boris had said, and Fumiko laughed. That was her name. Why did Sara remember the girl's name? Why not the friend's name?

A month after this picture was taken, Boris changed jobs. There was a big layoff at his agency, but he had already secured a position with Silver Canada. He took the severance pay, and they went to Cuba for two weeks. Varadero, of course. One day they took a minibus tour to Havana. A good-looking boy of about fifteen sat with them on the stairs to the old cathedral. Curiosity, nothing else. He talked about Hemingway, about poetry, recited Yesenin for them, in Russian. In the end he hustled them for five dollars. Sara gave him ten. Buena Vista people in every joint they entered. You walk in, five guys in the corner get up and start playing. They must be learning music at schools.

Sing when you're poor, play hunger harmonies—your government loves it. When they returned, Boris bought a new car, and then started the new job.

This one, what year was this? She and Johnny, interior, many people around them. They are both holding glasses. Johnny's face is shiny, it must have been after a concert. She is much younger. This must have been after the big concert at Tash Stadium—1986, the year they got together. She was still studying, but already working as a freelancer with state television doing offbeat reports on underground culture. Many naked legs in the back. Pretty women. It was difficult to defend her territory next to him. Women and public men. So predictable.

His right hand around her hips. Their sex at that time— madness. She was exploring, and he held the compass. Anytime, anyplace, anyhow. Was he in love in this picture? She still wasn't. She loved being with him, but not more than that. Well, yes, more: she was already buying clothes thinking of him. And he was clearing the place for her: there were still calls from other women when she was at his apartment, and he told a few of them not to call anymore. But was he in love? Johnny. Johnny.

She remembered when Boris stopped carrying the Pentax. "Tourists take pictures of a city," he had said. "And Toronto is our town now. Pointing your camera at a city means that you're leaving soon. It is distancing yourself, excusing yourself. We don't need picture postcards of our den. We have arrived."

The one she found next was closest to the "before" thing: Yonge Street. Mr. Satt's store in the background.

The street is covered in snow—only the tops of Sara's boots are visible. Luz and Sara are both laughing. It must have been during that big snowfall in the winter of 1993. Sara and one other girl went out to shovel, and since there was no one else around Luz came out to keep them company. Mr. Satt appeared, returning from somewhere. He took out his camera, and just when he was about to take a picture, the other girl slipped and fell into a big drift. That's why Sara and Luz are laughing. In spite of the snow, its calmness, its shroud, it is not a static picture. The two of them are caught in motion, their knees slightly bent, their bodies—in black coats—leaning against each other. Almost like sisters.

Later that same afternoon, that nice woman came in again—she purchased cameras for an independent production house and would regularly drop by to check on the new models—and she talked to Sara about coming to Toronto. She, like all the others, asked the same questions: Why did you choose Canada? Why did you come to Toronto? They wanted to hear praise for their country, for their city, they probably wanted you to say something they could take away and share as a moment of beauty or inspiration with their friends, but it was the wrong question— it has always been the wrong question. Because most of the time, the answer was banal. You had come to Toronto because someone you knew had come before you and said it was nice. Or the Canadian embassy in your country was the only one still giving immigrant visas. The right question was, and still is: Why have you stayed? But that's a hard one. Always a hard one.

No, here was the one she needed: She and Boris in front of their first building on Isabella. They are in their faded jeans and sweaters. There is no snow but it looks like a cold day—her hands are clenched into fists in front of her mouth and she seems to be blowing into them. Boris holds a cardboard box from which a teapot is protruding. They smile awkwardly at the camera, unsure whether to pose or not. Their neighbour took this picture. He was a transvestite from their floor, a large man who wore size 12 shoes and complained of trying to find a pair of heels to match his new skirt. He had just bought a camera that day, and wanted to honour Boris and Sara by shooting them on the first frame of the first film.

It must have been early November of 1993, just a month after they arrived. They had bought something, perhaps another piece of junk furniture, their hands were full and it was heavy, but it was sometime after five, a line of tenants in front of the elevators. A few people ahead of Boris and Sara stepped away when the door opened to wait for the next elevator. Sara and Boris did not think about it, got on, and saw that there was a man already standing in the cabin: he was in his early sixties, or perhaps younger because he was ill. He was leaning on a cane with some difficulty, and he asked them to press the button to his floor, which they did. They noticed that his face was covered in sores. The man asked, hesitantly, if they could help him from the elevator to his door. After they unlocked the door and led him to his bed, he thanked them profusely. Later, they overheard some other tenants: the old guy was dying. His lover had left him when he had first been diagnosed with AIDS, took off with their money, disappeared. In late November, a small note was pinned up on the tenants' board next to the mailboxes: the old man had passed away and, not being able to locate any friends or next-of-kin, management had decided to leave all his possessions in the recycling area. Tenants could help themselves. Boris and Sara picked out his china. The plates, cups, everything. They remembered something warm about the old man's appearance, something they wanted to keep with them through the winter of early immigrant days. That's when the transvestite shot that picture.

A summer photo next to the fountain in the Square of the Republic under a row of large square parasols. Sara is sitting at a table with Vesna and Gordana, the same women she was with when she met Miki. In fact, it was he who took this photo—he had come around the corner and taken the picture before they were aware of him. There are many empty glasses in front of them—they've been sitting for some time. One of them is holding her hair above her head with one hand. The heat. Sara is in a white tank top, leaning forward, the umbra is dark red, she is holding the tip of her nose with the thumb and index finger of her right hand, her mouth is open, she was saying something when the shutter clicked. Her left hand is on her temple. Together, her hands are hiding the better part of her face.

It was August of 1993. She and Boris had their Canadian papers, and she was starting the last circuit in that exhausting race towards their exit: saying goodbye to her friends. Yet, she wasn't doing it. When this picture was taken, it was very hot, a weekend, and Sara didn't feel like going to swim with about a million other baked bodies. She called her ex-colleagues from the television station, and they decided to visit the bookstore, maybe pick out something to read, and later cool off by the fountain, with some iced coffee and chat. But she wasn't saying goodbye, although she knew she would be leaving in a month, a month and a half. She did not mention her departure at all. Her fingers touching her nose, the other hand at her temple. Anyone who had ever read something about body language would read her pose easily: she was hiding something.

Her friends talked about the usual stuff that afternoon, about books, about politics, the latest city gossip, swimsuits, prices—standard nibbling of a hot summer afternoon. Around them, people lined up on the shadowy side of the street, shuffling their feet, pretending to look at the windows, careful not to expose any limb to the sniper of the sun. Only children ran out into the blaze, withdrawing immediately, their wounds now in need of an ice cream.

This was the city that Sara loved: smart, lazy, informed, misguided Belgrade. Gossipy, benevolent, slow-rocking city. This was what she knew she would miss someday. Still, she didn't talk about leaving.

Now, looking at that picture—Miki did not stay, he just wanted to say hi on his way to do something urgent, and later sent the print—she asked herself why. Her reflex answer was that she didn't want to draw attention to herself, she didn't want to hurt someone. It was her decision, and her suitcase to bear. But there was a deeper answer, and she had to face it now: she must have thought it was a temporary thing. Leaving for Canada was temporary—she would stay until the war rolled over into another country, then return to her proper place, her sun, her shadow. Words make something legitimate, they tend to drill into your memory. She didn't want to say the words.

If you want something to be forgotten, take a picture of it. If you want something to be remembered, tell it as a story.

Right, sister Luz? Is my world revolving around me now?

I've listened to you, I've found my mirror—my writing. My work changed everything, and they want me everywhere now. I don't even have to look for the news. I am the news. People love to hear a confession, everyone wants to be a priest of someone else's temple. Fine, I give it to them, I take my clothes off and I dance naked on the page. But was that such good advice?

When I stand before my mirror, when I read my articles, I see that the pages I have written are now writing me. I have nothing to confess anymore. I am empty now.

THE PATIENT. *October 30, 1998*

The ambulance stopped in front of the Emergency entrance, and the two men waiting there opened the back doors of the vehicle. The gurney was hurried through triage, the scans were done, and the unconscious patient was taken to the intensive care unit and hooked up to a respirator and a heart monitor.

The policemen who arrived a few minutes later gave the doctors the bare details. The patient was mounting his bicycle on the street when a car lost control on the slippery road and ran into him. The man hit his head against a lamp-post when he fell. The driver and the witnesses thought that he was dead, so he must have fallen immediately into a coma. The man had no ID on him and the police were trying to establish his identity.

The results of the scans came in. The unknown man had had his skull fractured on the right side. There were some cloudy areas in his brain, and the scans had to be repeated.

"This will probably make your life more difficult," said the doctor.

"Why?" asked one of the policemen.

"It could mean that his temporal lobes are damaged, at least the right one, and that almost always causes some form of amnesia."

For the next few days, the nameless man lay motionless. The nurses periodically checked his pulse and other vital signs, but there was no change. In the morning, groups of students would stand at the door while their professors talked about coma and types of brain injuries, moving nonchalantly around the bed, pointing at the numbers on the monitor.

His clothes had been searched in the meantime, yielding no identity papers of any kind, no membership cards, no bank plastic, not even a shopping list. There were a key chain, several banknotes, a few crumpled receipts from cafés and one from a shoe store, but visits to those places did not produce any leads. Only when searching the pockets again did they find another piece of paper. It was old, crumpled, and the handwriting was faded, so they suspected that the nameless man probably forgot he was carrying it around. It had found its way through a hole in his inside jacket pocket and was stuck between the pocket and the lining. It looked like a letter written in a foreign language, but it did not have any signature or date. The inspector photocopied the letter and sent it around, and the next day someone recognized the language as Serbo-Croatian. The inspector called the Yugoslav consulate, and a policeman in charge of security confirmed that the language was Serbian, and then translated it. It mentioned that its author was coming to Amsterdam, so the inspector presumed that the victim had written it. It seemed to be a love letter, a bit rambling, but it did contain something of importance—it referred to an event that the Serbian cop had heard of. In the end, he agreed to send a copy of the letter to his colleagues in Belgrade.

On the afternoon of the fifth day, a signal sounded at the nurses' station, and the nurse who ran in first saw the patient looking at the ceiling.

"He's awake!" she yelled over her shoulder as she went close. "How do you feel?"

He looked at her, his eyes dark and slow. "Non capisco."

"He's a foreigner," the nurse said to her colleague who just entered.

"It sounds like Italian," the other woman said. "I'll get Ornella."

The first nurse stayed in the room, waiting for the doctor and wiping the patient's forehead, rearranging the wires around his body.

"Dove sono?" the man said.

"It'll be all right now. The most important thing is that

you are awake, and that you rest. You have been in a coma for almost a week now, but you are going to be fine, nothing to worry about. Can we inform someone? What is your name?"

The man stared at her, then said, "Coma?"

"Yes, yes, the doctor will tell you more, I'm sure. Are you hungry?"

"Dove sono?" he repeated.

The other nurse arrived with the third woman, who smiled at the patient encouragingly and said, "Io sono Ornella. Come sta?"

"Dove sono?"

"In un ospedale, in Amsterdam," she said. "Come sta?"

He paused, sighed, and said, "Come un albero di trenta piani."

She smiled. "Le piace Celentano, no? Anche a me. Come si chiama?"

"Non ricordo," the man said.

"Ma bene. Ora viene il dottore," Ornella said, pointing somewhere behind the curtain.

"Bene. Sono stanco. Ciao bella."

"Arrivederci."

The doctor pulled aside the curtain. "Is he awake?"

"He is, Doctor," the first nurse said. "But he does not understand English. We thought he spoke Italian, so we called Ornella."

"And?"

"He doesn't remember his name, Doctor," Ornella said. "He speaks Italian, but—" She giggled.

"What?"

"Every other sentence is the title of a song."

THE REVERSE MAN. *November 9, 1998*

Tomo the Croatian nurse had a nickname at the hospital: the Reverse Man. When he came to the hospital looking for work, the first thing the woman who ran Human Resources noticed about him was that he uttered each name in reverse order—family name, then the person's name—as if reading from a telephone book. The social services had sent a letter of recommendation with him, saying that he was a refugee suffering from traumatic experiences. The head of HR took pity on him and hired him as a patient hygienist on the night shift. It was a smooth title for the rough job of cleaning toilets, changing sheets, and disinfecting bedpans. When he started working, the nurses noticed that he did other things backwards, too. Instead of pushing his trolley, he pulled it behind him. Instead of stretching a sheet over a bed first and tucking the ends in afterwards, he would straighten the bottom part, tuck it in, and then work towards the head part, as if a patient were already in bed and he was covering him.

Several months after he began to work at the hospital, he had his diploma recognized and could work as a nurse again. In time, his colleagues learned to like him, but they still joked behind his back. He was a subject of research as much as an employee. A famous anecdote went like this: Once old professor Van Dijk, leading his students on morning rounds, found Tomo in the corridor pulling a trolley, pointed at him, and said, "A thousand guilders to the one who comes up with the correct diagnosis for this man!" The students tried several guesses, but the professor kept shaking his head. Finally, when everyone had exhausted their ideas of possible disorders, Van Dijk said, "He's an exile, dear colleagues, an exile."

Six years after leaving Croatia in 1992, Tomo went back home for the first time. Everyone else at the hospital chose summertime or the holidays for their trips, but Tomo went in October. "I want to see my people, not the seacoast," he said. "In summer they are all elsewhere." He came back in a strange mood. Physically, he looked refreshed, but there were lines of bitterness at the corners of his mouth, and he scarcely communicated with his colleagues. Before his trip he had had a kind word for everyone he met, and his patients still loved him, so his co-workers let time heal whatever it was that needed healing.

The Italian—as they now unofficially called the name-less man—was moved from intensive care into his own room. Tomo was warned to be quiet and unobtrusive when he took over for the night shift, since the man had suffered memory loss and was still recuperating from the coma. Tomo pulled his trolley with prescriptions to the front of the door and stepped on the brake. He only intended to check on the patient to see if everything was fine. He tip-toed into the semi-darkened room, listening to the man's even breathing, and carefully approached the bed. Then he said, very quietly:

"You?"

· F O U R ·

LOVE OFTEN FLIES OVER LIKE THAT

FRIDIANS. *November 27, 1998*

The first snowstorm of the season was still raging. The wind had died down, and the snowflakes that the light caught drifting outside were the size of coins. Toronto had lost its edges, swaddled in cotton as if it had been wounded and needed some peace and quiet to recover.

Boris stepped back from the window and returned to his seat. Dinner was over and the remains of the dessert were melting on the platter in the middle of the table. Their guests slouched in their chairs, chatting the Friday night away. The radio was playing jazz.

"You two never argue," Selma said. "At least not in front of us. What's your secret?"

"Look at their eyes," Branko said. "They're calm. They don't give a fuck."

"We once had a big family dinner at our place," Nenad said. "I think it was my birthday, and there were three generations sitting next to one another. My granddad was about seventy at the time. He always impressed me as being calm and confident, but suddenly I noticed that his eyes were wide, as if he were staring at something horrific—he almost appeared insane. I thought it had something to do with old age, you know—shoulders bending, hips widening, perhaps eyes widening, too. I looked at my father and he had the expression too, but just barely. So I sneaked out to the bathroom, to look at myself in the mirror. I thought I was doomed: it had to be hereditary. But once I got here, to Canada, I realized what caused it: the slow grind of our old country. When you're young, a long way from the end, and your hopes are high, all doors open for you, you can do anything. Then you are middle-aged, and everything goes into slow motion. You go to work every morning, you get your salary every month no matter whether it was a good month or not, maybe they promote you, maybe they don't, maybe you have an affair with your colleague or maybe not, but there's nothing you can change anymore and new doors are not opening for you anymore because you chose that one door so long ago—and now what? You slowly acquire that look of horror in your eyes. It's not the fear of death. It's the horror of life, of looking back at it."

Branko was inspired to recite:

The stinking city opens its cheap joints
For workers who drink like dogs
Students without diplomas
Women without beauty
Homeless bachelors
Penniless travellers
Cheap music, heavy drinks

They fall for lotteries
I fall for horror.

"Fuck, that was a great song!" Nenad said. " 'I Fall for Horror.' Johnny."

"I still listen to it often," Branko said. He turned to his hosts. "You don't have any of Johnny's records?"

"No," Boris said as Sara answered, "We do," quickly adding, "But only in digital format, on my Discman."

Selma laughed. "Aha, this is a good time to start arguing, you two."

"Before Johnny," Branko said, "it was all 'I love you, you don't love me, I'm sad.' And then he came along, and the music was suddenly about street fighters, about desperate loners, about our balls stuck in the machine—about *us*."

"I have to admit that I miss that revolutionary feeling we used to have back then." Nenad took another sip of his wine. "We felt like we were the centre of the world. Now I feel sidelined."

"I am too full to start a revolution," Lila interrupted, and everyone laughed. "A little Pepto-Bismol and I could change the world."

"You'd need a megaphone, too. And a good dictionary," Sara added.

"And plenty of toilet paper," Nenad said.

"Speaking of dictionaries," Selma said, "we all learned English at school, but that version was so fossilized, don't you think? The other day I heard a piece on CBC, some guy doing a story about learning English. It was funny. The title was 'In My Language I Am Smart.' "

"That says it all," Sara said.

"You're the smartest one among us, Boris," Selma said. "You found a visual job. Good for you."

"Don't be so sure," Boris replied. "Even shapes need translation. Colours have different meanings. Once, they gave me some Christmas project to design. I made a palette of winter colours: white for snow, grey for buildings, and red for fire. A touch of ice blue. It looked good to me. But when my boss saw it, his jaw dropped. 'Where's the green? Where's the gold?' He did not realize that I had never celebrated Christmas back home, that I didn't share his colour code."

"Where's Johnny now, does anyone know?" Nenad said.

"I heard he disappeared when the war started," Selma said. "They think he quietly emigrated."

"Where to?"

"No one knows."

"We have at home that last album he did," Lila said, "the one that came out after he was gone. There's a ballad on it, 'The Mistress of Solitude.' 'Like the Mistress of Solitude she is pulling my strings.' Unbelievable song. I've always wondered who the woman who inspired it was. What the hell did she do to deserve such a song?"

Boris glanced at Sara, who was motionless.

"Oh, good, we're all Johnny's groupies here," Selma said.

Boris had met Nenad when he came to fix his computer. It turned out they had been working in different departments of the same company for two years, not knowing about each other. His wife, Lila, was also a programmer, though she used to be a high-ranking bank official in Belgrade.

Sara had found Branko and Selma in a bookstore. Branko, who had been a doctor back home, worked as a chiropractor, and Selma was studying to become a project coordinator in the software industry. The couples took turns hosting a dinner every Friday evening and they adopted the name Fridians for their group. Because of Friday, but also because of Freud.

"Children, we should be going if we don't want to sleep here tonight," Lila said.

They all turned to the window and stared at the white wall fluttering outside. Then everyone started getting ready to leave.

Half an hour later, with the dishwasher burping in the kitchen, Sara and Boris sat at the table finishing the wine. Usually, this sweetest part of their Fridays would start with one of them remembering something that someone had said, and then lead to a long conversation.

"I didn't know you brought Johnny's records," Boris said.

"I didn't. I found them all on the Internet."

He took a sip of wine and lit a cigarette. "I should tell you something regarding Johnny," he said.

She looked at him. "Why are we talking about Johnny now?" she said.

"We talked about him most of the evening, it seems."

"But not about the Johnny I knew. They talked about the public Johnny. The private one is my private thing, and it should stay like that."

They fell silent, both looking through the glass wall. A Dexter Gordon solo painted everything bluish.

"You're not offended?" she asked.

"No, but do you miss him?"

"Boris."

"Do you miss him?"

"I ask myself what happened to him. Don't you?"

"What happened to him is what happened to all of us," Boris said. "We had a life, the war came, we lost that life. We chose new identities and started again. Here, some- where, anywhere else was good."

"New identities? You think he's hiding somewhere?"

"Hiding? Only in the way we are all hiding. But—no, that's not what I meant. Look at the Fridians. We all used to be something else back there. But we hide it on our résumés. Overqualified? Dangerous. Remember Sasha's interview in that theatre magazine? He claimed that he had single- handedly invented political theatre in Serbia, spitting on all those who came before him. The first banned theatre show there was in 1954, when Sasha was only a spermatozoid. He knew that not one of us would send in a correction. Why? Because we all lie a little. White lies, small stuff, but still— nobody draws a clear picture that would unite here and there, now and then. We think people here would not believe what we had and what we had to give up to emigrate. Others lie just because they can, and it's tempting. Witnesses are few and far between, and most people just don't care."

Sara got up to walk to the window. She stood there, looking into the whiteness. Boris continued his soliloquy:

"This woman claims she was a well-known actress in Belgrade—we know that she was a junior producer in one of the theatres. But apparently she has always wanted to act, and now she is recreating her history in order to achieve her goals. That's what hypnotizers do: they advertise themselves well to make their audience more susceptible. Actually, that's a good metaphor for what we do: we hypnotize—others, but ourselves too."

Sara was still silent. Boris remembered what this was about.

"Johnny is probably in Amsterdam, hypnotized into doing something new, as are the people around him."

"Amsterdam?"

"Or not. But Amsterdam fits."

She nodded slowly.

"Perhaps he's not into music anymore. In fact he can't be, or we would have heard about him. He's apparently not into anything that draws attention. But I'm almost certain that he's alive and well. Maybe even happy, I don't know."

"Happy?" Sara said, her back facing him. "Are you happy, Boris?"

He walked slowly to her, glass in hand. He was tipsy but not drunk. He hugged her.

"That's a scary question, isn't it? I'm not doing any art, so I'm probably not screaming with joy. But I'm with the woman I love, and we are not bad as a team, and that gives me happiness."

She did not lean her head against his shoulder, although Boris thought this was the perfect moment to do it. He removed his arms, slowly, and stood beside her.

"Remember that night in September, when we first kissed? I've never asked you this, but—should I have cancelled that cab? Should I have stayed that night?"

Silence.

Finally she said, "I've always liked that you decided to leave, how you didn't want to take advantage of the situation."

"Do you love me, Sara?"

Silence.

"Do you?"

"Sometimes I do. But it all gets blurred. You, me, Johnny, the war, Toronto, Belgrade, all of it."

He kept silent for a while. Then he said, "Well, that's probably the best I can hope for."

She heard something in his voice, something that nobody else would, and put her palm on his shoulder.

"This snow will cover the whole world," he said.

LOVE AID. *December 23, 1998*

It was only a pattern on some silver foil, green salted with white schematic flakes, just a roll of cheap wrapping paper that she saw in the window of a drugstore, but it was enough to trigger Sara's usual December melancholy. When she was a child, her parents would start bringing home presents long before the New Year's tree would be standing in the corner of their living room. They would buy something on their way home from work and wrap it up in their bedroom before adding it to the pile. Her parents communicated most of the time in short, economic outbursts—this needs to be done tomorrow, you have to finish your homework by seven, we are going to Dubrovnik this year—as if too many words were a sign of bad manners. Thus, never sure what the others wanted, they never went for a single present.

When they were at work and the housekeeper was going about her usual chores, Sara would sit on the floor of the living room, staring at the stack of presents wrapped in colourful paper, spending hours trying to guess what was in each one, who bought it and who it was for. She knew early on that there was no Santa, but that only made her love the holidays more. Her parents' usual fits of arguing would abate towards New Year's Eve, and her family would enter some sort of ceasefire, where small errors would go unnoticed and the bigger ones, the ones that would normally prompt hours of quarrelling, would be noted but not addressed. If this wasn't love, it was as close to love as they could muster.

After her parents had separated, Sara lived with her mother in their old apartment and—although the tree would still be positioned as usual—the whole magic of guessing was gone. Sara was eighteen when her grandmother died and she moved into her now-empty apartment on her own. Every December she would get two large parcels, one from her mom and one from Munich, where her father lived with his new wife. The boxes continued to arrive after she emigrated to Canada, always in those few working days between Christmas and New Year's. Although her parents continued to pack many presents into their boxes, collected into a single package it felt like a one-time affair.

"They could parachute their parcels as well," Sara once said to Boris. "Love Aid."

This December was not helping her mood at all. Nothing bad was happening in their life, but the city was gloomy under heavy skies that always promised but rarely delivered the virgin white coat. She read somewhere about a special sun lamp, made for curing the sadness of dark winter days, but she could not bring herself to imagine that a small light bath would trick her brain into feeling chirpy again. The Canadian winter started too early, was too harsh, lasted too long, and covered all the beautiful bodies for months, making everyone a puritan. She could cope with cold, sunny days, the ones that—when they came—lifted her to a mountain in her imagination, or maybe to the porch of her father's cottage back home. The sky of molten lead was dangerous for her.

She tried sex as a cure. One week in particular: she shaved her pubic hair, walked naked around the apartment, sucked the whole space into her vagina and put it out like a juicy summer fruit, stroked and sucked Boris a few times a day, fucking to find a path to the other side of gloom, but it did not work well. The more he filled her with his dick, the less strength she had to defend against emptiness.

One day in mid-December, walking in the underground streets at Yonge and Bloor, she ran into her old colleague, the Romanian clerk from Mr. Satt's video store. She told Sara that Luz was in hospital, but she did not know which one. It was rumoured that she had attempted suicide. This was not a revelation—anyone who had met Luz knew suicide had always been there as an option—but it contributed to Sara's fund of sad thoughts. She thought of calling Mr. Satt and asking him where his wife was, but rejected the idea as too insensitive. Calling hospitals one by one? Not practical.

Unusually early, two days before Christmas, Sara got a parcel from Belgrade. It contained several presents, and she almost missed the envelope lying at the bottom, half-hidden under a flap of the box. She found three pieces of paper inside. The first one was a letter from her mother. It was not long: her mother was fine, she was going to travel to Slovenia with her current boyfriend to meet old friends for New Year's. It ended with a question: did Sara recognize anything from this strange letter that she attached? A clumsy police inspector had brought it to her, asking for her help. He did not have much hope, but thought he'd ask, an international request, he said. He thought that Sara should see it because it mentioned certain events Sara had helped organize. Can you imagine that? They actually have records of your moves and dare to admit it? Really. However, the police would appreciate it if Sara could help in any way, because the poor man who wrote it had amnesia from a blow to the head, and they did not even know his name.

Sara unfolded the other paper. It was a facsimile, two pages, with an additional faded stamp registering it as from the files of the Belgrade police. She recognized the tiny, dense handwriting immediately.

Love often flies like that, imperceptibly over the evening and into the night. A quiver on your lips, a look over your shoulder, and caution until the next meeting. Reason withdraws before the temptation to forget.

A few days after I arrived here, I walked into a café that sat where the ocean meets a canal. There were no other customers there. The girl at the bar made me an espresso and I sat outside, on a balcony, looking at the ocean foaming in Amsterdam harbour. It was a grey, windy day, and the surface was of steel and anger.

I couldn't take my eyes off it. After all the summers I had spent on the coasts of Montenegro, Dalmatia, Greece, Spain, soaked and choked with the coconut smell of sunscreen and postcard villages, I suddenly realized I craved grey seas, dramatic skies, and imposing ocean liners.

Strange: I expected that peace would be in order. I expected to be drawn by a monastery, a vow of silence, strings of words handwritten on parchment, and here I was, struck by this rage and thunder. It was law and anarchy in one, beauty and horror, salvation and danger. This was not a lascivious, senseless, naked sea. This was a partner, a philosopher. This was life.

I sat there thinking, wouldn't it be great to sail this ocean? To remove myself from the stolid solid ground, and go where everything floats, and rises, and falls, go where the wind makes the streets and sharks mark the numbers?

Now those streets are between us. Now I am on that ocean and, look, everything floats.

I could not call you directly, you do understand that. Boris probably has told you everything about my being at war, so you must have known that they would tap your phone, trying to get me. For the same reason,

I could not call him. Instead, I contacted my old drummer, and dictated a letter for you and one for Boris. I hoped that at least one of the letters would find its destination, and that you would come to Budapest. ~~My drummer told me you never picked up your phone, that he was certain you had moved.~~ He ~~also~~ told me that he left a message in Boris's mailbox. Boris must have read it. I told him I would be in the Mátyás Hotel after two o'clock on March 7. I was there from ten in the morning. Instead of flying in that day, I could not wait, came to Budapest by train the night before, and took a room near the station, usually rented for short loves and long regrets.

It was a chilly day, with fog that cloaked the morning and made it very secretive. It was not Budapest anymore, it was Casablanca—then again, every city with the sounds of war in the distance is Casablanca, my dear Ilsa. ~~When coming to Budapest I was daydreaming on the train. I saw you and me alone on a deserted street, back to back, the two of us against everyone. After all that had happened, I was certain that you would be the one to understand, that you would be on my side no matter what. The more people I met on my journey, the more I loved you. As the sea of ugliness expanded, you became a taller island.~~

Around two, the fog cleared. ~~Around two you were married to my best friend.~~

~~There is nothing I can do now, except send you this letter. You have chosen, and you've chosen well. I knew that Boris was in love with you. He never told me that,~~

~~but I knew the way we know it's going to snow by the way the air smells.~~

That there was a woman with me in the apartment when I came to pick up my stuff and run, you probably know by now. She saved my life, I saved hers, and then we went our separate ways. I don't have an explanation. There is always something you can say to defend yourself, but I stand naked before you. There was a war, there were people dying, there was death waiting for me as it waited for all of us there, but still I am not saying that death explains everything. Fear is an umbrella, fear is collapsible.

~~After I played that concert that you and Boris organized, in the Square of the Republic, my life became a heap of twisted metal. I was still inside, sitting among blood and rust and sharp edges, trying not to make a move. Then I realized I was dead anyway, and decided to get out. I was not sure what to do, except try to talk to you.~~

I did not belong in that room by the station. A long love and not a single regret.

Love often flies like that, imperceptibly over the evening and into the night.

I wish the spring in your heart to remain alive. I wish you to succeed without me.

Sara and Boris celebrated New Year's with the Fridians and two other couples at Lila and Nenad's house south of the Danforth. All was fine. They watched Das Neujahrskonzert from Vienna on January 1, as always. All was fine. Sara flew away from Toronto the next day on a plane to Amsterdam. Boris was still asleep when she locked the door behind her. On the table in the living room, she left a copy of the letter her mother had forwarded.

SILENT MOVIES. *January 3, 1999*

Sara's mother had tracked down the hospital through the inspector who had given her the letter. As soon as Sara's train arrived in the heart of Amsterdam, she took a cab there. The driver, a man with a turban, kept talking quietly in a foreign language through the headset plugged into his mobile phone, and she was grateful for his lack of curiosity. She had been to Amsterdam a long time ago, travelling with her friends on an InterRail ticket, and she had good memories of the city. She watched the crowded streets while the driver fought to get to the ring road. When he sped up she leaned back.

What would she say when she saw him? She did not think about it during her eight-hour flight. Before boarding the plane she took a sleeping pill, and she did not even remember takeoff. They woke her twice, once for dinner and once for an early breakfast, and then they landed. Still sleepy, she had an espresso in an airport bar with tropical palms, but it wasn't enough to wake her up. Never mind, she loved this strange state of consciousness, between dreams and reality, behind worries, ahead of sorrow.

When they stopped, the driver did not disrupt his telephone conversation. He pointed his finger at the number on the meter and she gave him a bill.

The winter day in Amsterdam was a joke compared to what she had left in Toronto. She flew out of minus twenty-seven Celsius and landed in a balmy plus four. She pulled her suitcase behind her through the hospital entrance.

"I'm here to visit your patient Johnny Novak," she said at the reception desk. "He has recently been moved from intensive care. You might have him as Milan Novak."

"Are you related to him in any way?" asked the nurse.

"I am his girlfriend," Sara said, and quickly added, "If it's him."

The nurse looked at her. "He's in 1013, that's ward 10 West. Follow the yellow signs. If you recognize him, you can confirm his name, okay?"

Sara nodded. The woman took the details from Sara's passport and showed her the way to the elevator.

The door to room 1013 stood open. Sara paused in front of it, brushed the hair from her face, and entered. The room was in semi-darkness. The blinds were drawn, and the Amsterdam sky was gloomy. She leaned her suitcase against the wall by the door and waited for her eyes to adjust. She did not dare look straight at the man's face. The whole installation around the bed made her shiver. Wires and tubes hooked into different parts of the body: a puppet. The strings around the figure lying motionless will go live any moment and the being will sit up. The Mistress of Solitude clenched her fists and slowly went towards the bed.

His skin was colourless. His eyes had shadows around them. The stubble on his chin made him look helpless. His hair was still long. She reached out and touched his hand lying on the blanket.

"What are you to him?" said a quiet voice from the door. Sara flinched. "His girlfriend. I used to be, that is," she whispered back.

"So you know who he is?" the man asked.

"Yes. His name is Milan Novak, but everyone knows him by his nickname—"

"Johnny. Finally. I told them who he was, but they didn't believe me." The man came into the room. He wore a nurse's uniform. "My name is Tomo," he said.

"How is he?"

"He's better than he looks," Tomo said. "But let's talk outside. He won't be waking up soon. They are still stuffing him with medicine."

"There is nothing about him that interests us, other than the missing persons part," the inspector said. "His name is not in our database. There seem to be no suspicious circumstances related to his injury, so we're closing the case. In short, he's not a criminal, and this was not a case of revenge."

"Can you tell me what you did find out?" the doctor asked. "Maybe it could help with his recovery."

"Novak entered the Netherlands in February 1993. He came from Germany, where he applied in our embassy for refugee status. He didn't have his passport at the time. He said he had to enter Germany illegally, because he was a deserter. A temporary visa was issued to him—at that time the expedited procedure was in place for such cases— so he was legit when he came. He went through the usual stuff: learned the language, was given an apartment, and then he started working at the Film Institute. They gave him a job classifying old reels. His colleagues told us he was always nice to them, was always punctual and efficient, never caused any trouble. He kept to himself, but nothing suspicious."

The doctor shifted in his chair. "For two days he spoke Italian only. Now he doesn't understand it. Is there anything related to Italy in your notes?"

"Nothing."

"Are there any names? Any particular friends or significant others?"

"Novak was good to everyone and close to no one. If you ask me, another immigrant story. Not yet adjusted. I mean, we could give you the names of his colleagues, but I don't think you will find a name that would help any more than the others."

"With these things one never knows."

"I'll tell my men to fax you the details."

The inspector closed his notebook and stood up to leave.

"Inspector?"

The policeman raised his eyebrows.

"We have a man here who claims our patient was a rock star in his old country, very well known . . . " the doctor said.

"We checked with his colleagues here. Nobody ever heard Novak play or sing. He never showed any interest in music." The inspector flipped a few pages in his notebook. "Ah, yes, this is sweet: he mostly worked on silent movies."

———

"Nothing."

"Not a single memory?"

Johnny remained silent for a while, looking at the ceiling. His eyes turned back towards her.

"I can't find anything. Your name means something, but I can't relate your face to the name. The name is in a good place, but I don't know if it belongs to you or to someone else with the same name."

"I've told my mother to send me some photos of us together. She has a few."

He thought for a while. His face got cloudy. "This must be painful for you. I'm causing pain for the people who knew me. I'm sorry."

"Don't worry about others, Johnny, just work on yourself now."

"Sara?"

"Yes?"

"Is it worth remembering? People tend to think they had an interesting life even when it wasn't. Pain, love, lust—it happens to everyone. I mean, maybe I'd be better off not remembering. Apparently, I am in some sort of a new life. Should I leave it at that?"

Was it selfish of her to remind him that she used to be his girlfriend?

"I don't know that anyone ever perceived the loss of memory as a blessing, Johnny. But that's not the answer to your question. I can only give you my version. Was it an interesting life? Very. Were you creative and respected for it? You were. Were you hurt? Who wasn't? We came from a country at war. There are no untouched people there."

He was leaning against the pillows, his long fingers slowly drawing an invisible map on the sheets. Many curves. He was not looking at her.

"I remember my childhood. The movies I watched, the books I read. The friends I had. I remember Caspar Hauser, and the term 'feral children.' But there is no you, or that other guy you mentioned—Boris?—and there is nothing about the war, and I don't know how to play the guitar. I don't remember the music you say is mine. Tomo played some songs for me. They sound like something I could have written, I suppose, because they obviously talk about my childhood, but they're a little too light for my taste. And the music sounds odd."

"That's not so strange. You would probably write those songs differently today."

"That's not the point. Why are you not in that picture? Or that friend of mine?"

"Johnny, there's a letter you wrote to me, but you never sent. They found it with you when they brought you here, and I got it a few days ago. In that letter, you mentioned that Boris had heard the whole story about the war. From you. We can call him."

THE PIGEON. *February 12, 1999*

However much she wanted to see Johnny's apartment, there was fear, too. What if he—among other memories he had lost—had forgotten that there *was* a significant other? He could have been married, maybe there was a child. Maybe his family was on Mauritius and would be coming back in a month. She took the tram to the Spui square and sat inside the Café Luxembourg, drinking double espressos and mineral water, for an hour and a half. She might have ordered another round had she not become so jumpy from caffeine.

When Johnny's doctor told her it might be good to bring something from Johnny's apartment and show it to him, something that might be significant, she agreed, provided, of course, that he was fine with it. They went together to 1013, and the doctor repeated his idea to the patient. Johnny said okay, but there was a moment of hesitation, a pause long enough for Sara to notice.

She remembered that pause as she tried his keys in the lock of the narrow house off Spuistraat. A dark secret? Something she should not see? There were several keys, very similar to one another, and she tried them one by one.

"What are you doing?" said a man's voice behind her.

She jumped. "Isn't it obvious?"

"Well, yes," the man said, "but I don't see why someone would risk breaking into my apartment in broad daylight."

She stared at him for a few seconds, opened her mouth, closed it, looked at the number on the wall, and started stuttering apologies. The man laughed. He was blond, with freckles on his face, in jeans and a sweater that hung on his bony shoulders. He held a supermarket bag in his hand.

"I should have kept my mouth shut," he said. "It would have been nice to come home and find you there."

His switching to a different mode somehow angered Sara, as if his role was limited to comic relief and he had overstepped his boundaries. She did not answer, but turned away and walked next door.

"Are you going to Novak's place?" the man called after her. "I haven't seen him in a while. Where is he?"

"He's in the hospital," she said. "Are you his friend?"

He scratched his head. "I don't know, ask him," he said. "But we had a couple of beers together. Nice guy. Are you his sister?"

"Girlfriend."

"He found you in a hospital? Which hospital is that?"

She smiled.

"Seriously, what happened to him?" The man came closer.

"He was hit by a car, and was in a coma."

The man whistled through his teeth.

"But he's okay now, except that he has memory loss." She remembered something. "Have you ever been in his apartment?" she asked.

"Once, for a few minutes."

He wouldn't know if there was a particularly important object. "Did he live alone?"

"You mean, did he cheat on you? I never saw anyone else going in. He was always very quiet. I've never even heard music from there. Do you need help?"

Well, at least that. "No, thanks." She fumbled with the keys again. Finally, the right one. She turned it twice.

"Nice meeting you. Tell him Kees wishes him well."

"Thanks, I will."

She locked the door behind her and climbed a steep, narrow staircase. At the top she entered his living room. Then she realized it was the whole apartment, except for a small bathroom in the corner. A tall window without a curtain looked out at the house across the street, and underneath it was a large old writing desk. A small monitor sat on the desk and next to it the skeleton of a computer, an open structure full of wires that connected different boxes. Although it was apparently an old machine, probably found on the street, Johnny had it covered with transparent plastic. A small hotel towel lay over something on the desk, very likely the keyboard, and some wires led to a small plastic synthesizer on a stand next to the desk. A narrow foam mattress on the floor in the corner. The walls were densely covered with pieces of paper of different colours and shapes, all containing drawings and words. With strange, sharp lines on them, they resembled parts of a large map of an unknown city. There was no single picture pinned anywhere. The kitchenette was basic. A dirty cup in the sink, the coffee remains in it dry and cracked.

The apartment contained only essential stuff, except for the computer and the instrument next to it, and even they were humble. It felt monastic.

She crossed the room, opened the window, and looked outside. She could see a canal on the right at the end of the narrow street.

She returned to the desk and lifted the cover. Yes, a keyboard. She pressed the switch on the front of the computer and the machine started waking up. That synthesizer meant that he was making music, after all. While the computer was starting, she opened the closet. She recognized only an old jacket. Several shirts on each hanger, layered like onionskins, and underneath them, folded jeans. She smiled—still the same—and with a jolt she recognized the real reasons behind her fear of coming here: she had a key to Johnny's apartment again.

The cards on the wall were not what she had hoped they would be—some sort of a scrapbook—and for a moment she felt disappointed. She started reading some of the inscriptions, and they looked like snippets of a movie script. The drawings on some of the cards were a storyboard. Johnny had no talent for drawing, but she could still recognize silhouettes and street scenes.

The desktop on the computer finally came on. She sat down and looked at the screen. There were several program icons, and several video links. She clicked on one of them, named "immigrant bird."

It must have been a very early reel, as the picture was slightly jerky, with noticeable scratches, and all the movements on the screen were a bit faster than normal. The silent movie opened with a wide shot of a promenade, somewhere on the French Riviera, it seemed. The men were mostly in light-coloured jackets, almost all of them wearing straw boaters. The women, strolling with light parasols, wore elaborate hats and long white dresses. People were friendly to one another, frequently stopping to exchange pleasantries. An automobile would pass from time to time. Seagulls were scattered here and there, frightened of people, landing hurriedly to pick up a chunk of something looking like food and immediately flying back to one of the boats or towards the sea. Oddly, there were no pigeons in sight. Except for one, close to the camera, that was doing the senseless things that pigeons do: walking around, taking a shit, picking in the dust. Suddenly, the voice of a narrator came on, as if it were the inner voice of the bird.

"Look how tiny I am, sir. I am but a grain of sand on your shores, never to travel farther. I am the sudden raindrop that fell into your quiet lake. I am the dust in your eye, sir. I am collectible. Do you know any other pigeons from my war-torn country?"

Another voice, booming, official, belonging to a moustachioed man in a top hat who had just appeared before the camera:

"PLEASE FILL IN THE NAME OF YOUR COUNTRY OF ORIGIN ON THE DOTTED LINE. USE CAPITAL LETTERS AND WRITE IN BLACK INK."

Sara looked underneath the desk to see where the sound was coming from, and realized that the sides of the desk were actually two large speakers.

The pigeon continued:

"I am the embarrassing sound that your intestines make during the monologue in a theatre. Bear with me, and I shall pass. Pretend that my feathers have no colour, that my brain is flat, that my beak utters no sound. I will stand in front of your cathedral, with my lesser god at my wing, waiting for your mercy. Your border is a rainbow, and I'm starting again, anew, alive. Tears and mucus have the same salinity."

The pigeon flew several yards away and landed on a bench by the water. Mechanical sounds started filling the space, giant machines at work, marching bands, boots hitting asphalt—all mixed together—and the pigeon's voice suddenly became a hiss, full of scorn, whipping from the speakers:

"I am the giant penis on your morning horizon. The sun rises behind my glans. There will be thousands like me. I am that horde that will topple your temple. My voice is before your Jericho." Boom, boom, boom, boom. The sound stopped. Blank screen.

Sara stared at the monitor for a while. Is that what Johnny was doing here—making soundtracks for silent movies?

She stood up, her hands shaking, probably from too much espresso, and looked around. She was here with a task. The task was to find something that might unlock Johnny's memories. But what? She went to the group of cards that she was reading earlier and started taking them down one by one. There was nothing else she thought was significant.

She had the key, but it unlocked a new door.

Tomo spent much of his time around Johnny, far more than what was expected of him. He brought him fruit, old music magazines, some rock recordings from Yugoslavia on his old Walkman. She should have been grateful, she knew that, but she wasn't. The problem was that he was not the type one could comfortably argue with. Tomo never raised his voice, and at every sign of conflict, or even nervousness, he quickly withdrew. Yelling at him would have been like shooing a sad puppy.

Except that he wasn't helpless. On Thursday, Sara brought some fast food with her, burgers and fries she wanted to share with Johnny. Tomo saw her in the corridor,

---

recognized the paper bag, caught up with her and told her that high-fat food aggravates the symptoms of brain injury. Before she could even answer he held his hand out, took the bag, and threw it into a trash bin in the hall.

On Sunday, she rearranged things in Johnny's room. She thought it would be nice to make some changes, no matter how limited, and moved the chairs around, repositioned the vase and pushed his nightstand a little forward. On Monday, everything was back in its original place.

On Thursday, Sara brought with her two posters she had bought in a small bookstore down the street from where she was staying. They were good reproductions of some peaceful Flemish landscapes. Johnny liked them and she taped them to the wall. On Friday, the posters were gone.

The idiot was not even supposed to work on Fridays. Everything until now had been emendable, snippets of bad dialogue that could be fixed with a little tact, but this was too much. Sara marched down the corridor and knocked on the frame of the open door. There were two women in the staff room with Tomo. He wasn't in his uniform.

"May I speak to you for a second?" she said.

"Sure." He followed her out into the corridor.

Halfway to room 1013 Sara stopped. "Did you remove my posters?" she asked. Her voice was low and harsh.

He shrugged. "Yes. They are on my desk, I'll bring them right away."

"Why do you have to change everything I do? And don't tell me it's hospital policy."

He looked straight into her eyes. "Technically, it is," he said. "But that's not why I did it."

"So why, may I ask?"

"For the same reason I moved the furniture back, Sara. He needs things to remain predictable, boring if you wish. He needs coordinates. You think that changes might do him good. They won't. If he's going to be successful in his search for the past, he needs to not think about his present."

"But a landscape can't hurt—"

"I agree. And I don't agree. But seeing that you are angry with me, let me tell you something: we are working on the same thing, you and I. As much as you want to bring back his memories, I do too. Well, maybe not as much." He smiled faintly. "But in any case, we are on the same side."

She looked carefully into his eyes. "What is your interest in this?"

"Interest?" He seemed to measure the word, to taste it: bitter. "I don't have any interest."

"Why, then?"

He looked at the floor for a few moments, then raised his head. "I fell in love with my wife while dancing with her to one of Johnny's songs. We played it at our wedding. We had all his records when we moved in together. She had the ones I didn't."

He paused. Sara waited.

"She was killed. A grenade hit our building. I was in the basement, getting some food. And it was fired from our side. An accident, they said. The fire destroyed everything. If he doesn't remember his songs, I'll . . . I'll teach him, note by note."

LAVA. *March 8, 1999*

The beginning of March brought longer days, and a sense of optimism, fluttering on the sunrays that entered the hospital, crisscrossing the corridors and rooms and poking the pale skin of the patients. Sara thought there was the smell of spring in the air, but she wasn't sure. Not here—this air was foreign.

The cards from the apartment did not help at all. "Probably because they are the product of his abstract thinking, not of his experience," the doctor said. Her mother ("You should have known that you were the most significant thing in that apartment, dear") started sending her magazines from Belgrade, and Sara read them to Johnny whenever she could, hoping that some names or places or even words would trigger another memory in his brain. And it worked, to some degree. Sometimes he would ask her to repeat a sentence. A few times he recognized the locations and then recovered some of the lost pieces related to the particular sites.

"It's International Women's Day," she said, entering his room that Monday morning. "I brought you flowers."

He smiled. "You look happy today."

"I am," she said, putting the bouquet on his nightstand. She kissed him on the cheek—for some time now she did this whenever she arrived; he didn't object, and it gave her a sense of normalcy. She noticed that he had shaved and smelled of . . . "What is it?"

"What?"

"That perfume."

"Oh, it's an aftershave—Tomo gave it to me."

"Can I see the bottle?"

"It's in the drawer. Why?"

She took a black bottle out and smiled. "He must have discovered that detail somewhere."

"What detail?"

"That's what you used to wear back in Belgrade. That man will marry you in the end."

Johnny laughed. "I asked him the same when he gave it to me. He said that my legs weren't to his taste."

She went to the sink to fill a vase with water, checking herself in the small mirror above the sink. She looked good today. Not the same person as she was in Toronto, but this one was okay. Back at his bedside, she unwrapped the flowers.

"I was thinking, Johnny—you know, it's difficult to retrieve the memories of our hometown. And it has nothing to do with your particular state. Belgrade is so different from what we remember. It's not even about us never being able to stand in the same river twice. Belgrade is not even a river anymore. It's flowing, all right, but more like lava, burning everyone in its way."

"What's lava?"

She looked at him and saw his smile. "Don't frighten me, mister."

"Sorry." He kept smiling. "What took you there?"

She stopped for a second. Where? Toronto? Or Boris?

"In your thinking. Why did you think of Belgrade?"

"Oh. I read this article about gangsters dying one after another," she said, arranging the flowers in the vase.

"There was a documentary, *See You in the Obituary*, where they interviewed some gangsters about their life and work, and three of the interviewees were killed during the filming. The article says that the assassinations have continued. The theory is that these guys were used by the regime for some hush-hush activities, and now the secret service is getting rid of them. Do you remember a guy they called the Candyman?"

She glanced at Johnny, and saw his face darken.

"What about him?"

"Well, he was the night itself. Before the war, he always operated abroad, keeping his hands clean in Yugoslavia, at least on the surface. The story was that he was a contract killer for the secret service. Then, when the war started, suddenly he had his small army. They operated in Croatia and Bosnia for a couple of years, then he disbanded the unit and they lived happily ever after. The official stand was that the state didn't have anything to do with his army—he was a private citizen and free to do as he wished. If he wanted to help his countrymen under attack, that was up to him. If he wanted to buy tanks with his own money, who could prevent him?"

She sat next to Johnny, looking straight into his eyes.

"And?"

"And he was killed a week ago. On the street. By several attackers, in two black Audis, in broad daylight. His bodyguards were killed, too."

Johnny covered his eyes with the palm of his hand, then moved it slowly up his forehead and all the way to the back of his head.

"Does something ring a bell, Johnny? You remember the war?"

"I can't. I can't."

She leaned over and hugged him. He hid his face in her hair.

"It will come, Johnny."

"I know it will."

"Are you afraid of your memories?"

"Aren't you?"

"I have an idea. If I get you a notebook, maybe you can write down what you remember from the period closest to the empty zone. Go to the very edge, Johnny. I've read an interview with some writer where he said that writing in his notebook made him concentrate better and retrieve some memories he thought were lost. He thought it was something related to the economics of handwriting. Too many moves involved just to erase it and start over. Will you do it, Johnny? Will you try? But you have to write up to the edge, because maybe then you will see what fills the void."

He seemed confused.

"What?"

"What will I write about?"

"Anything. Make it like a diary."

He leaned back a little, still letting her hold him.

"Sara?"

"Yes?"

"Do I still hurt you?"

"No, Johnny. You never did. I hurt myself."

PURE WHITE LIGHT

CHANGE. *April 15, 1999*

At first, after Sara left, Boris found solace in his work. He stayed late, fixing every hairline of his designs, changing colours even when he was certain they were already right, pretending to be the perfectionist he never was. He left his office only when he felt that he would be able to eat something then fall asleep on the sofa in front of the TV when he got home. One night, crossing the street, a cab almost ran him over. When he heard the screeching of brakes, he lifted his head and realized that the light was red and that he was in the middle of the street, his brain on automatic pilot, his senses dead.

He also knew that the feelings deposited quickly in him, layer upon layer, were starting to choke him. He had read enough about psychoanalysis to realize the danger.

So he changed his tactics. He started taking long walks in the evening, usually ending up at the lake, where he would have a whisky by the water, in Spinnakers, and then take the subway home. If exhausting himself at work meant filling his brain with such an overload that he did not even have the time to think, this was the other extreme. Emptiness crept into him, shrouding everything in both his inner and his outer worlds and threatening to render his entire being invisible. Gazing at the lights from the islands across the harbour one evening while sipping his whisky, he saw his reflection in the window. His shoulders were slumped, his hair in disarray, his left hand propping his forehead.

Was he looking for oblivion? He could never forget Sara or Johnny. It wasn't an affair, it wasn't someone else's life. It wasn't the stuff of books or movies. It was in his veins, tattooed on his skin. There was no line under it all, and there couldn't be without all three of them meeting again and talking it through—or fighting it through.

He glanced at his reflection again. That man looked like he needed a change. There was no storm swirling around him. A storm leaves hope—shaken, beaten—but still hope. This was dead water. This was some place with no current, no wind, with dead fish floating around him, naked trees on the shore, no sound at all. He needed a change. Deep, thorough, unconditional change. He had thought his life had changed enough when he emigrated.

But when, exactly, did he lose control? At what point did he switch to automatic pilot? He had been in command back in Belgrade. And when he had decided to leave. He was still driving when they came to Toronto, when he found a job, when they bought their first car. Or was he? Was their coming to Toronto the last conscious step he took, and everything else just an automated process, something that this big-hearted country offered like a mother to all its hopeless, confounded, clumsy new children?

Change.

Then change it would be.

He spent the last few days of February and the first week of March sorting through the closets. He carefully separated everything into three heaps: one for the garbage, one for Sara, and one to be stored. In his old notebooks he found many sketches for projects, ideas he never had the time to follow through. He unearthed old letters, pictures, boarding passes from their flight to Toronto, a photo of the two of them—and some others—standing with a Mountie in his screaming red uniform immediately after they got their Canadian citizenship. Shopping lists, napkins with doodles on them, two old notebooks that contained his early diaries (abandoned at fifteen, when his father found them). Sara's early pictures with Johnny, both looking beautiful, her photos (now seriously fading; she should scan them) from her primary and high schools, rows of girls and boys in blue uniforms, letters of hers that he did not want to read, love letters to her from some boys before Johnny, and a small pressed branch of pine. He held that branch, surprised. There were two tiny cones on it, and by them he recognized the branch: it was the one he gave Sara that fateful night on the mountain, when all was clear and maiden and white. He started crying. He went to bed in the early-morning hours and slept the next day—it was Saturday—until one. When he woke he felt rested.

————

In March, serious speakers spoke in serious voices about bombing Serbia. At first, Boris thought it was just a form of political pressure, as did his mother, as did all her friends. But the General, his mother said, was sombre about it. His contacts had said this bombing was going to happen.

He still felt the need for Sara, but, surprisingly, he discovered that it had shifted into a craving for their talks, not for her body, her touch. Recognizing that he again needed the shelter of his mother tongue, Boris started seeing his Serbian friends a lot. They had all entered the zone of high anxiety, some hoping that the coming war would mean Milosevic's demise, some beside themselves with anger at the whole Western world. They were not able to discuss anything: the heat of the situation had switched off the analytical parts of their brains. The language was there, but there was no communication. There were people around him but he was not among them.

Then, on March 24, in the early afternoon, he was sitting at his computer designing a web site for some company when a colleague who was married to a Serbian woman entered his corner office, his face grave. "It's started," he said.

Boris remembered later that he had asked, "What's started?"

Days at work. Most of the people around him were full of understanding. His boss gave him small tasks, leaving him a lot of time to follow the news on the Internet. Some faces were hostile, some jerks with their tiny, steely smiles asking how he was, pretending not to know. Only a few, though.

He spent evenings in front of the American consulate, demonstrating with a few hundred, sometimes thousands, of other desperate, quiet people. In the early days, Boris was reserved, standing on the side, smoking, listening, a small target on his lapel. One evening, a vehicle belonging to CTV News drove by and someone in the front seat opened the window and gave them the finger. They drove slowly, as if they were brave, as if they were righteous. There were hundreds of police across the street, armed, on horses, with dogs. Boris finally felt rage. He bought a Serbian flag the next day—and increased the number of pills he was taking.

Several nights later, he decided not to go to the demonstration. The world was crumbling, fast, but he felt he could face it better alone. He rented a cabin at a small hotel on a lake a few hours north of Toronto and drove there for the weekend. The lake was grey, the food was shameful, the town reeked of perversions and suicide. Or maybe it was him. He spent the first night reading, tried to find a prostitute on the second night, and drove back to Toronto on the Sunday, more tired than when he had arrived. At home, he unplugged his TV and at work he deleted the news bookmarks on his computer.

In the second week of April, he decided to start a new artistic project. One Thursday evening, he sat with a coffee and a cigarette, opened his Moleskine notebook, and took up his favourite pen.

He had seen a picture at the beginning of the bombing, of the night sky over Belgrade. The anti-aircraft artillery gave it everything they had when the first bombers approached. They fired thousands of grenades, rockets, and bullets towards the invisible enemy. The planes returned fire. The majority were tracers—red lights from NATO ammunition meeting green lights fired from the ground. The picture also caught the explosions on the outskirts, and, together, the lights created a festive atmosphere. It was the joyous beginning of slaughter.

The light.

Religions love light. What if we are only parasites in some unimaginably big being, which doesn't care about us because it hasn't had its regular checkup yet and does not know that we even exist? And even if it did, it would love to get rid of us and feel good again. Can we communicate with it in any other way except by sending it pain?

Can we, humankind, be of any use in this universe? What is the cost of our existence? If energy is finite, than our devouring of it must mean that some other life form, somewhere, is dying, or perhaps has not even had the chance to be born. On the other hand, we ourselves die, and return our elements to the earth after borrowing them. After we die our ideas live for some time, then melt into the big stream of history. The palimpsests receive another layer. Perhaps, after a deafeningly long silence, and after travelling through space, our elements turn into another life form. Perhaps we are everything before we are born, and we will be everything forever—peaks on an electrocardiogram whose length is the sum of time. We are light itself. We are

Pure.

Why does almost everyone who has had a near-death experience talk about the white light at the end of the tunnel? The white of wisdom, of purity, of the divine, of all colours united. The white of surrender, of cowardice, of cold. Six thousand five hundred kelvins. The white of ghosts, of death, of weddings.

White.

He looked at three words on the sheet of paper before him, and it was obvious. A wall of pure white light. The cure for sadness. Diodes, then. What triggers them? And what happens when you pass the wall? No, that was too far. Okay: sensors can trigger a change of colours as a visitor approaches the wall, from something subdued to blinding white. And when he enters the portal in the wall, he finds . . . a new identity. A new language, a new name, a distortion of the old one, a new life in some distant country. New sounds, new smells. Exile. There will be a glass box on the other side. A heavenly cage. Visitors can come from the other side, too, and observe the person in the cage.

Feverishly, he started jotting down plans, adding words here and there, arrows curving from the side towards the pentagram in the centre of the page. White noise, of course. On this side. On the other, silence.

He was happy when he stopped working that night. At the office, he continued during the breaks, and then back at home, the next day and for the rest of the week. The excitement of a fresh idea. From the outside, he looked as if he were talking to someone sitting next to him. He paced the room, gesticulated with his hands, frequently combing his fingers through his hair. When he stopped, he felt hungry. Going to the kitchen to make something, he caught his reflection in the mirror. Greasy hair, dark circles under his eyes. He smiled. Every time he looked really ugly it was after creating something beautiful.

White as in White City—Belgrade? Perhaps not.

Over the weekend, he shaved his head and shaped his stubble into a goatee. Change it will be. It had been three and a half months. Sara was now coming to him only in short bursts of pain.

WITHHELD. *April 19, 1999*

Once, a long time ago, he had read somewhere that the ancient Slavs believed that Tuesday was the best day of the week to start something. They hated Mondays. Ignored them. Pretended they did not exist. Boris liked the idea so much that he chose to adhere to the principle.

So, when Monday came, and he felt his Light project was unfolding well, he called in sick and took his Moleskine for a walk. In the Beaches, he bought a coffee in a plastic cup and went for a saunter by the lake. The air was cold, but there was no wind. He found a bench, zipped up his leather jacket and sat there. The lifeguard tower was to his left and the downtown skyscrapers in the distance to his right. He watched seagulls fight over some food. On the edge of the dog's off-leash area, there were several stone totems. He had seen a guy making them once. A large rock balancing on top of a small one, another on top of it, another and another. It looked nice, but it wasn't art. It was the guy's personal cure, perhaps, but it meant nothing to anyone else, except as a curiosity.

His cellphone rang. Boris pulled it out of his pocket carefully. He did not want to answer it by accidentally touching a key before seeing who was calling. The screen said "Withheld." That usually meant an international call. He pressed the button and said, "Hello?"

There was a short pause. "It's me."

Boris's body reacted before his brain did. He put his cup down and reached for his cigarettes. "How are you?"

"I'm fine. You?"

"Where are you?"

"In Amsterdam."

"What . . . Where are you staying?"

"I found a room in a house full of students from Belgrade. It was okay before the bombing started, but now it's like Noah's ark. Every day somebody else's relatives arrive. How about you?"

"Me? I'm in the Beaches. Didn't feel like working today. I've begun a new project."

"That's good. Something promising?"

"We'll see. For now, it helps the coffee go down. Any news from Belgrade? Is your mom okay?"

"Yes. I talk to her every day. Did you hear that they killed dozens of Albanians by mistake?"

"Yes. I can't worry about them, though."

"No."

Pause. Two seagulls started to fight.

"Boris?"

"Yes, love?"

"Don't call me that. Please."

"Sorry."

"Take care of yourself. Seriously."

"How is he?"

"I don't know. He has memory loss. Selective. Otherwise, he's fine."

"Selective?"

She hesitated. "He can't remember you and me, and he can't recall what happened during his time at war."

"Shit. Shit. Can he play?"

"No."

Pause.

"I've shaved my head."

"Oh, god."

"No, it's good actually."

"Okay then."

"Can I call you there?"

"I'll keep my Canadian cell number for another month."

He wanted to say "love" again, because that's what he felt. She said goodbye and hung up somewhere in Amsterdam. He stared at the phone in his hand for a while, then put it back into his pocket. It was sad and good. Or would be good. They would all meet again, and it would be different, but they would talk again. It will be as it used to be. Love is nobody's fault.

He was unlocking the door to their apartment when the phone rang again. "Withheld."

"What did you forget?"

"Boris, it's me, your mother. Did you get my telegram?"

"What happened?"

"Your father, Boris. He's dead."

"Are you hurt?"

"It wasn't a bomb, Boris. He fell off a horse. Thank God, he didn't die in bed. He went like a true soldier."

"When is the funeral?"

"We'll wait for you, but you have to hurry. Boris, I know it's hard to come now, and be careful, but I won't be able to get through it alone."

"I'll come, Mom. I'll check the flights right away, and I'll let you know."

"Please, Boris."

"Don't worry, Mom. I'm coming for sure."

SOMETHING ELSE. *April 20, 1999*

He had a plane ticket for the evening of the next day. He called the bank to reserve enough cash to cover the unexpected and scheduled a pick-up for the next afternoon. He packed that night, throwing just the necessary stuff into his old brown bag. The next morning, he forced himself to sleep in, called work to tell them his father had died and that he was going back for the funeral, and then went to the bank. It was just past three when he had finished everything. He returned to the apartment and made a coffee. There were at least three hours to kill. He was surprised by how efficient he was, and how fast and clear his thoughts were. And then he had an idea. Something else that could be done, something that could not wait. He took several blank sheets of paper from the printer, and his pen, and lit a cigarette. He would send it from the airport, after he finished checking in.

Note: The speed of thoughts
Once, in Belgrade, I was in a car with my friend and thought that I was going to die. It was a very cold winter. The two of us needed to travel south to a small town where we were to meet with a gallery owner and talk about an exhibition. The roads were covered with ice. My friend thought of postponing the visit, and suggested we call the guy instead, but I needed to see the space before I could talk about the details. As a compromise, we agreed to leave around noon, and return the next day. The midday temperatures should have been warm enough to melt the ice.

For the first forty miles everything was okay, and then we stopped in the service lane so my friend could scrape the ice off the windshield. He opened the door, put one foot on the ground, and, as soon as he tried to stand, fell down beside the car. I realized later that this should have been a serious warning, that we should have turned back right away, but we were both laughing so hard we could barely catch our breath. We continued driving. On a bridge, a few miles later, a sudden crosswind caught the car. It swerved to the left and the right and then started to spin. Fast. The ice was so slippery that there was no traction at all, and the steering wheel was useless. The wind continued to push us as we spun, and at one point it became clear to me that the car was going to hit the railing on my side.

Fortunately for us, our front right wheel hit a thick layer of dirt and salt and snow, and it slowed the car down so much that it came to rest, almost gently, against the railing. After the collision, a truck zoomed past. We sat there, trying to comprehend that nothing bad had happened. We turned on the engine again, and carefully drove off the bridge.

Only when I was back home did I realize how fast my brain was working in those moments when I thought I was going to die. From the moment when I saw the railing approaching until the actual crash—it must have been only a second, two at the most. But in that blink of an eye, my train of thought went something like this: "Oh, we're going to crash on my side. There is a big truck approaching. I hope we'll be off the road by the time it gets here. Look at that railing—it's probably made of steel and the side door will be crushed, which means that my ribs are going to be broken. Not too many of them, I hope. What if my right arm breaks? Am I going to die? Shit shit shit! Here we go."

Until then, I had considered all those stories about the movie of your life flashing in front of your eyes just before you die to be one of the legends related to death, but on that day, I started believing it. If only I could think like that all the time, or at least more frequently. That was a thousand times better than cocaine. If only I could think that I was dying more often.

—T.O., April 17, 1999

RETURN. *April 22, 1999*

Strange, there were no birds at all.

Miša must have fixed the engine in the meantime, because he started revving it. He should go back. Or maybe Miša would pick him up. The engine roared now—he will choke it like that. No, he will let the bus come to him. What is Miša doing? The roaring was going up and down, up and down, and it was very unpleasant, alarming. Perhaps Miša needed help.

Boris turned around to see that Miša was still by his minibus, waving towards the city behind them, beckoning with his other hand.

It took Boris several seconds to understand that what he had heard was not the engine of the small grey bus. It was an air-raid siren.

For a minute or two nothing happened, except the wailing of the siren. His driver was waving dramatically with his hands. His gestures made no sense to Boris. He wanted to shout that there was an imminent air raid, that they should get off the bridge—they should run back.

That's what was wrong with his idea: running back. Back to what? Bombs could fall there, or here, or over there. Back there was the city, on the other side the old fortress. Would they bomb a monument?

Boris looked towards the checkpoint at the entrance and didn't see any police. They must have gone. The wind carried another noise with it, a heavy boom from afar. The way it spilled over onto everything suggested that it had come from the sky. The bombers. He looked up and saw only a few large clouds.

A wave of fear swept over him. For an instant he felt like running, no matter where, just running. Then he made an effort to control his thoughts. If the enemy wanted to destroy the bridge, they had to hit it in the middle, where he stood. As long as he wasn't in the middle, he should be okay. He started to walk quickly towards the fortress side. Behind him, he heard a barrage of anti-aircraft fire. He turned to look. The planes were now visible. They flew in formation at a very high altitude. Ominous birds moving south. For a moment he thought they would fly past to hit some other, less fortunate town. Then, as he watched, squinting, one by one the planes made a sharp turn to the right, increased the distance between them, and headed towards the city.

Boris started running. There was no time to think of sides anymore. He just ran and it happened to be in the direction of the fortress. The first explosion, somewhere behind him and to the right, was so powerful that he expected to be blown off the bridge. He half turned as he ran to see if something had been hit, but there was nothing in his view that betrayed the target. It must have hit something far away, Boris thought, but then how come the sound was so murderous?

Seconds later, another bomb hit, and a surge of thick smoke rose in front of him, from behind the citadel. Several more explosions sounded in the distance. Now under the second arch, Boris began to slow down and, after a few more steps, stopped. He leaned against the rail to catch his breath and looked all around. The minibus seemed deserted. There were pillars of smoke to the south, to the east, and one somewhere behind the city. The place where he stood was as good as any other.

"I'm not thinking fast," he said aloud. "I'm not dying."

This thought echoed in his head for a few seconds, then it made him stretch his lips in the beginning of a smile.

From where he stood, he could see several vehicles on both sides of the river moving fast. Were they trying to escape being hit? How did the city look from a plane? Like a grid of virtual buildings, with depersonalized small dots running around? A hundred points for hitting that building, ten for that other one, minus fifty for hitting a hospital, and you get demoted if you hit an embassy. But if you hit fifty running targets, or three suspicious, fast-moving vans, you get a new life. With three new lives you enter God mode.

Boris lit a cigarette and started coughing with the first drag. Coughing is good, nobody ever dies from coughing, or sneezing, or farting. Excretion is life. He spat over the rail.

Mice. We are like fucking mice.

When the war started, in 1991, life was suddenly reduced to survival. Get food, get some money, stretch both to last as long as you can, fuck fast, don't draw attention, keep the old medicine, oil your network, and run, run, run. That was because of Milosevic. Now you get these idiots with their humanitarian bombing. Stash food, keep it fresh, run into shelters, store water, batteries, medicine, and run, run, run. Don't plan, don't expect, just stay alive. Postpone everything. What was there between the wars? Another country, another continent. Peace, prosperity. But: you don't know who you are, or were, you feel like a rough stone in the pocket of a silk suit, you fight for your language, you miss the old and crave the new, and you can't imagine your future. The homeless on the sidewalks scare you, they are only one step away from you, and each step you take could be that step. Find a job in that virtual building—fifty points. Buy a house—a hundred points. A new car—thirty. Get married to a citizen—a new life. But in this game, merely living gets you minus points. You're working against time, all the time. If you just stand there, your joystick still, your mouse sleeping, you lose a life in the end.

And for what? Once replanted, will you have longer branches, greener leaves? Will the new worms be gentler to your roots? For what, all that effort? Do you live in Moscow now, dear sisters? Did he finally arrive, Vladimir and Estragon? Running to save your life, to save your soul? Define soul. Define your life. If your soul consists of your beliefs, your principles, your feelings and memories, is it not the same everywhere? Does your life not consist of your people, your private geography, your imagination? Then it is different every morning, no matter where you go. Your steering wheel is useless. You are what you run away from. Flick the switch on the lights that cure sadness and glue your ass to the chair.

"Fuck you," Boris whispered. "Fuck you all."

Old Macdonald had a camp, e-i-e-i-o. And in that camp he had exiles, e-i-e-i-o. One was wounded here, one was shattered there, here a shit, there a shit, everywhere is shit shit. Old Macdonald had a camp, e-i-e-i-o.

Several groups of planes were now flying in different directions, at different heights. The bombs and missiles made a well-rounded thud, while the anti-aircraft guns produced cacophony. The fox had entered the barnyard, and the hens and turkeys responded with their staccato of fear. Tracers flew in all directions, although it was still daylight, and thick rolls of smoke rose in the distance. The city raised its roofs and church towers high, spiteful and angry, and there was the mighty, rolling river beneath his feet, two elegant arches above him, the old fortress on the hill above. Fury attacked peace with all its power, but peace stood proud. The General would have been happy to see this. Someone should be taping the scene—if there are enough blank tapes left after the previous wars.

Johnny had erased Sara and him, like a tape that did not contain anything worth watching again. That's all right, Johnny, I have a copy of that tape. That's all I watch.

Boris finished his cigarette and flipped the butt over his shoulder into the river. It will be less *schön*, less *blau*, but who cares. He turned his back to the city and started walking towards the fortress, his hands in his pockets. There was less smoke ahead than behind him. When this was over, he'd wait for his driver on the citadel side. He looked towards the clock tower on the hill above, and stopped for a moment, confused. Then he saw that it was close to four. It was perhaps the only clock in the world whose long arm pointed to the hours and the short one to the minutes. That was because minutes were not important when they had installed it.

High above, a plane appeared from behind a cloud and almost immediately dove to the right, firing two missiles at the two-arched bridge.

You have legs, so you have to learn to walk, and keep walking. And you have hands, so you have to keep touching. And you have love—must love. And eyes, must see it all. Smell, hear, lick, fuck, penetrate, inhale, exhale, inhale, exhale. The change, the trip, the meeting. We are energy, we don't exist, nothing does. We are nothing but movement, just a vibration. Pain is irrelevant, pain is just energy gone astray.

Birds: that's why the birds have disappeared, they had a premonition about the bombs. You're an artist, Boris, you're supposed to see the details, you stupid shit.

Four seconds later, two almost simultaneous explosions shook the bridge under Boris's feet. He started running again.

Another plane high above him dove towards the river.

When a powerful explosive device detonates, the first thing that happens is the devastating shock wave, blowing everything away from the centre, torching and tearing apart. But the explosive burns the oxygen in the air, creating a strong vacuum that, for an indefinably short period, draws everything towards the centre of the explosion. The bomb kills and then hugs.

When our senses become saturated with sensation, they send a hasty signal to the brain that they have encountered something white. White noise, white light, white ghost, the white of God. White is all colours, and we are not capable of dealing with anything "all" at one time. White is the colour of defeat for the senses as it is for warriors. It is the colour of the end, and the colour of birth.

Most things in nature experience a moment of hesitation between their appearance and growth—revolution, eruption, flower, idea, child—but this glow immediately expanded to obscure the world around it. It came from a spot on the bridge in front of Boris, and at the very moment it appeared, it grew until it had devoured everything. It was white. Pure white. It was inevitable, inescapable, it was like the right word. He was still running when it had appeared. There was something majestic and horrible about it, like the declaration of war, like shards of metal tearing a body apart. The flash cast a long shadow of his body across the asphalt and metal bars behind him, a silhouette that—in the same breath—broke into thousands of little shadows. For a brief moment it seemed that all these particles wanted to join together again as they were sucked into white, and then they found their way between the bars and concrete and melted with the surface of water.

In a little while, the sirens sounded the end of the air raid. When the smoke had cleared, the old bridge was still standing, though there was a wide fracture in the middle of the left arch and two smaller cracks in the right one. The small grey bus was leaning to one side. The sun shone on the river below, and a big fish—drawn by the light—made a full somersault right below the fracture. The clock on the tower on the Petrovaradin fortress was showing some time after four when the birds returned to the bridge.

THE NIGHT IS NARROW

FARTHER. *May 6,1999*

"I had an abortion, Johnny, in March 1993. I was already married to Boris. I missed my period in December. I wasn't sure I was pregnant, but I had missed it in November, too. I was a mess then. You had been gone since November, and there were problems everywhere, war and all, and my whole body went nuts. When the test was positive, I thought it was yours, Johnny. Then they told me the dates, I looked on the calendar, and realized it couldn't have been, so I went to the hospital."

Sara was sitting on the chair by the window. Her voice was flat. It sounded like it was coming from a shortwave radio, with the occasional crackling and some words inaudible because of Johnny's sporadic "Mm-hm." He looked like he was sleeping. But Sara was not sure about that. There was almost nothing now to be sure about. Boris, Johnny's future, her future—everything was in the air. She had no map in her head, no backup plan. All she knew was that she had to resolve this, here, she had to stay and hear the verdict, and that decision had to come from Johnny.

She did not come to Amsterdam with that plan. When she had read Johnny's letter, her first reaction was fury at what Boris had, and had not, done. Getting on the plane in Toronto was a gesture of revenge—one big swipe at erasing all the years of guilt. Mother, Father, Boris—this is my fucking life, watch me now. Even Johnny—he could have tried harder. Of course she wanted to help him, but she did not know then if there was any love left. So many things had happened. She looked different, sounded different, she thought in another language. She would come, and help, and see what happened.

"Miki. You remember him? The war correspondent? I don't know why it happened. It was only once. I felt bad the next day, I felt awful. I'm not saying this was because of you. I hated myself for doing it."

She paused. "Hmm. Interesting. A few years ago I would have said, 'For allowing that to happen,' but not anymore. Nothing just happens, Johnny. We do it all. It is all us. But you know that. You said that destiny was your lover. God, Johnny, what a song that was. Even if there were only that one song, you would still have to come back and sing it. You can't just forget it. That tune is so true. So many others we grew up with were lies. 'I hope I die before I grow old'? So why didn't he? I thought a lot about it in Toronto. We got our citizenship a day before my thirtieth birthday. I didn't know what to make of it. I mean—it's good, you have a passport, you are free. But immigrants don't really need passports—they travel mostly to their old countries, anyway. And then I realized it was a sign. It was not a passport for borders, it was a passport for the future. It said, 'Thirty is good, don't be afraid of it, it's still you. Forty is good, sixty is good, life is good.' "

She stood up and stretched.

What had changed her plans was her visit to Johnny's apartment. Inside were traces of the old Johnny, but there were also signs of another man. A man who was strong enough to cut off the links to his amazing past and start something completely different. A man who had so much art in him that it had to spill out, in any way possible. A man whose apartment had no signs of other women. A man she knew so intimately from somewhere so distant that it might have been a dream. That visit had changed everything. She liked this new, old man. He seemed to like her. Let's see what happens. But under one condition: we will erase the word "again." Nothing will be again, nothing as it was. You have no memories of me? Fine, here I am—start making them now.

She looked at him, and smiled.

"I was thinking—maybe we could go to Toronto. Once you get out of here. It's far enough. Toronto is good, you would like it. It's strange when you see it at first. You expect it to jump at you, the way the big cities do, but it just sits there, waiting for a hug. You could play your music, write books, or record your soundtracks—whatever you want. I'll get a job with a magazine. We could travel. I've always wanted to see Canada from coast to coast. I want to visit Alaska. And Japan. Let's go far, Johnny. Nothing ties us to

Belgrade anymore. We are strangers there, Johnny. We're strangers everywhere. Isn't that fantastic?"

Out the window she watched as a solitary man walked towards a narrow canal holding both his hands crossed at the back of his head. Delight or despair? Sara sat down again.

"And—don't jump now—I think we should sit down and talk, Boris, you, and me. There are shards all over the floor. We won't be able to step safely until we clean them up. There is nothing to be continued, that is impossible, and we can all go our separate ways after we meet, but we owe it to one another."

Johnny moved again and his cover went astray. She stood up and tiptoed to his bed. She leaned over to straighten his blanket. Just as she turned to go back to her chair, she felt his touch on her hand.

"Stay," he said.

"How much did you hear?"

He turned on his back. "Enough."

"The abortion?"

He nodded.

"There is something very important I want to tell you. Sometimes I know why you're here, sometimes I don't," he said.

She opened her mouth to say something, but he raised his hand.

"I just wanted to make something clear: if this is about guilt, you can go."

Standing at the head of his bed, she looked into his eyes. She fought back the tears, and won.

FIVE CELLS. *May 7, 1999*

It was so unusual for a patient to receive a letter in the hospital that they misplaced it as soon as it had arrived. It was only after the hospital administrator came back from a short trip to Brussels that the envelope was discovered on his desk. People pretend that a stay in a hospital is just a temporary lapse in logic, something that passes in the blink of an eye. Or vanity lets them think that the only thing a patient needs is their personal visit, a bouquet of flowers, a box of chocolates. But isn't an old-fashioned letter perfectly suited to patience, and the patient—that appropriate title that so efficiently displays the impotence of doctors? The administrator was pleased with his philosophical stance, and, with these thoughts in mind, he decided to personally deliver the letter. There was no room number on the envelope, just a foreign name and the name of the hospital. Come to think of it, it was surprising that the letter had even got here. He checked the date on the postmark: it had been sent from Canada on April 21, and it was now May 7. Oh well. He found the name in the database and headed to room 1013. The patient was sleeping when he quietly entered. He left the envelope on the nightstand and tiptoed out.

Tomo drew the curtains aside. The man in bed moved his head a little but did not wake up.

"Johnny?" Tomo said. "Johnny?"

The man blinked, then opened his eyes. "What time is it?" he said. His voice was hoarse.

"Time for lunch, Johnny. You've slept enough."

"They gave me those pills again."

"I told you, Johnny, they had to do it before today's measurements. They needed to make sure no unnecessary worries inflicted your brain waves."

Tomo helped him sit up, and propped the pillows behind his back.

"They've been keeping me here forever. I want to go."

"Soon, Johnny. Soon, I promise. Don't argue with the doctors. By studying your case they can help others. That is good. The unit here that deals with brain injuries is world-renowned. You've talked Italian, and you've never been to Italy or studied the language. They have to make sure you're not going to slip into that again, or something equally unpredictable."

"If it's about the unpredictable, they'd have to keep me here forever."

Tomo smiled. He removed the tray from the trolley and helped Johnny position it in his lap. Then he sat on the chair.

"I brought you something special today," he said after Johnny started eating. He pulled a book from somewhere inside his hospital uniform and held it up. "Look."

He put the book on the bed in front of Johnny and returned to his seat. Johnny was still very sleepy and it took some time for him to take the book and look at its cover. He continued to chew, looking at the picture on the jacket.

"Good photo, isn't it?"

"Not bad."

"It's just been published. Your new biography, Johnny."

"Great," Johnny said. "Then I don't have to remember anything. I guess it's all here."

"No, Johnny, you have to. You have to. I flipped through it. Some parts of it are bullshit—they don't like some of your songs that are really beyond their comprehension—but they do go into detail about your eleven concerts in a row in Kulusic, and they have some really good photos from your work with Pankrti. I didn't know anything existed from that period. Did you?"

"I kind of remember that there was a photographer around. Some tall guy. Blond. Yeah, Canon."

"Very good. He had a Canon."

"No, it was his nickname. He actually had a Hasselblad and his name was Krstulovic. But they called him Canon because . . . I can't remember why. Shit."

"No, no, that's good, very good. See? It may be just a trickle now, but it's coming. What else can you remember from that session? Were there any girls around?"

"Was Sara in while I was asleep?"

"I don't know. I just got here."

"Wait, what day is it today? It must be Friday. You don't work on Fridays."

Tomo remained silent. Johnny continued to eat, flipping through the book.

"Sara is very pretty, man."

Johnny looked at him. "Yes, she is."

"What is the problem, Johnny? You can tell me."

Johnny sighed and let the book to close itself. "She loved someone that's not me anymore. I don't know who I am now. I don't know who she is."

Tomo thought for a while. "Does that really matter, Johnny?"

"Of course it does."

"But she's here, every day. She's by your bed even while you're sleeping. She helps you shave, and wash, and eat. She loves you. Whoever you are now, she loves the new you."

Johnny did not say anything.

"Don't you like her?"

"A lot."

"There. That's all that matters. Is that a letter?"

Johnny turned to the nightstand and took the envelope in his hand.

"Why does Tomo want to refresh my memories? Why is it so important for him?"

"He is fighting for *his* memories, Johnny," Sara said. "If *you* don't remember, so many things in *his* life will be lost. It would be as if he had lived an illusion. There's been a war, people have been displaced. Some of them didn't even bring pictures with them. Their friends are dead or far away. Your music is one of the few things that tie it all together."

"Isn't that an overstatement?"

"Do you have any idea how many people would be lost if someone erased the Stones or the Clash from our memories?"

"Was I that important?"

"In that space we used to call home—yes. You were that important."

He looked at her face. Sara was serious. She sat on the edge of his bed, touching the watch on her left wrist with the fingers of her right hand. He had seen her every day for the past few months, enough to know that something was not right today.

"Still, he can be strange."

"You have no reason not to trust him. He's done so many wonderful things for you. Did you know that he actually bought it?" She pointed at the guitar propped up on the other side of his nightstand.

"He said he had borrowed it. I asked him to take it back."

"He bought it. A nurse told me. And he doesn't even play the guitar."

Johnny looked again at the instrument, and slowly nodded.

"Listen, maybe you can learn how to play. You were good once, maybe you can do it again."

Johnny moved to sit up. She leaned forward to help him, but he stopped her.

"Oh, god, I didn't tell you the best news. They're going to publish your book!"

"What book?"

"Your diary. I sent a copy of your notebook to one publisher only, because I knew someone working there. And they thanked me for that. They want to speed it up. They don't want to wait until the war is over, they want to publish it now. Much more material is needed, so you have some work to do."

"Isn't it funny?" he said. "My memoirs are being published while I'm trying to regain my memories."

She looked at him, pursing her lips approvingly.

He sighed. "Did you know that there is no such thing as selective memory loss?"

"Says who?"

"Take a look." He reached underneath his pillows and fetched an envelope.

Sara opened it. She recognized the handwriting.

Boris wrote:

Apparently, some psychiatrists claim that the whole idea of selective memory loss was invented during the Romantic period, probably by a writer. That the brain could erase certain memories in order to better cope with trauma was a clever invention, don't you think? For the arts, maybe, but not for reality: if that were true, wouldn't we all be walking with hammers in our hands, hitting ourselves over the head all the time?

If this idea about Romanticism is correct, and it seems that it is—there are no traces in literature, medical or otherwise, of this notion prior to the 1800s—you'll have to work harder. You can drill through that pain you carry inside. Nobody knows what happened to you. You told me some of it the last time we met, but the feelings cannot be passed on. They can only be described, their external shape sketched. When we say "love" we mean "circle," when we say "pain" we see a wedge, but how sharp that wedge is or how wide the circle, we have no way of knowing on the outside.

If I say that I have always loved Sara, deeply, even when she was with you, what would it change? If I say that you are still my best friend, will you believe me? I have no means of persuading you. Except for this deep, crusty scar on my heart. My love for her and my love for you fought each other while you were around. Later, I lost control. That is all. I can't apologize, because how can one apologize for love?

I am begging you to remember.

Sara was never really my woman. She leaned on me because it was rough, and because you were not around. Remember that, too.

Your music kept us sane, before and during and after. If you take that away, you take so much. Remember it.

If you were particularly good at something, it was fighting. You fought the bans, the police, the regime, you fought against all odds, and you always won. Fight again.

Fuck the war and me. Let Sara love you.

B.

She cried like an expert, without a sound. Her head was bent a little to the left, her shoulders rounded. The tears from her eyes fell sideways, towards her ears for a brief moment, before they returned and gathered in the corner of her mouth. She had no makeup on and the wet path was clean, clear, and shiny. She put the letter in her lap, and continued to cry as she looked out the window. It was raining outside again.

Johnny touched her hand very slowly, very lightly. Five cells of his fingers against five cells of her skin.

"They called me this morning, Johnny. Boris is dead. He was killed during an air raid on the bridge to Belgrade."

The door opened quietly. Johnny turned slowly and saw Tomo. The Reverse Man stood there, not sure whether to enter, because he saw Sara's tears. There was an expression of pain and confusion on his face, a silent apology. Johnny nodded his head for Tomo to come in. When he was still hesitant, Johnny pointed at the guitar. Tomo picked it up and handed it to him. Johnny put his fingers around the neck, pressed down on the strings, and hit them with the nail of his right index finger, sliding his left hand at the same time. The sound that came out of the wood was like a scream.

ACKNOWLEDGEMENTS

All of the characters in this book are real: they live in my head. Any likeness to people who do not live between my temples is coincidence. While the historical frame for the events described in the novel is rather accurate, I had to resort to some compression. For example, the conference on Yugoslavia at Innis College in Toronto was held later than it happens in the book. Some of the events in the war section did take place, but not in that area, or during the period, described. And the village where Johnny ends up was not modelled on any existing community.

There are four people I wish to thank here. Having them on my side means so, so much. In no particular order:

When I needed Joanne Mackay Bennett's wit and wisdom while writing this novel, she didn't ask any questions, she just helped.

Anne Collins is my editor at Random House Canada. Her laser cuts deep and cures manuscripts without leaving scars. Her passion for books is unrivalled. It's an honour to have her as a friend.

Behind every one of my books there is a woman. Silvija

Jestrovic is behind this one. It was conceived one night during one of our conversations after our daughter, Ana, had fallen asleep. She is the warmth.

Branimir Štulić is a poet and a fighter whose work keeps inspiring me. His poems have taught me that words are not only units of language, but drops of blood that keep this world alive. Some of his verses have provoked a few of those "quoted" in this novel.

Finally: this is a night book. Parts of it were written on two continents, in five different cities, on five different computers, two of which died in the middle of the work, almost taking down the manuscript with them. Some snippets were handwritten in five different Moleskin notebooks, and on a Palm T | X. The original synopsis for the book was dictated into a telephone. But all of this work was done between 10:30 p.m. and 2:00 a.m.

DRAGAN TODOROVIC is an award-winning author, broadcaster, multimiedia artist, poet, musician, and theatre director who grew up under Tito loving Jimi Hendrix and Tom Waits. He emigrated from Belgrade to Canada in 1995. While he is currently living in England with his wife and daughter, he considers Toronto his home.